# RULER OF THE SEAS

*—An Admiral's Diary*

## Book 1 of the
## Tidal Pool Trilogy

Brick Tower Press
Habent Sua Fata Libelli

**Brick Tower Press**
Manhanset House
Shelter Island Hts., New York 11965-0342
Tel: 212-427-7139
bricktower@aol.com • www.BrickTowerPress.com

**Library of Congress Cataloging-in-Publication Data**
Mazzella, Donald.
Ruler Of The Seas, Book 1 of the Tidal Pool Trilogy
p. cm.

1. Fiction—Historical—20th Century—World War II. 2. Fiction—
Romance—Suspence.
3. Fiction—Sagas. 4. United States—Fiction
Fiction, I. Title.
ISBN: 978-1-59019-007-4, Trade Paper

December 2023

# RULER OF THE SEAS

—An Admiral's Diary

Book 1 of the
Tidal Pool Trilogy

**Don Mazzella**

Dedicated to the most persistent,
wonderful person I know,
my wife, Joann Mills Laing

and

Doreen and Leonard
who proved love happens at any age.

Also by Don Mazzella:


*The Janus Principle*
*An American Family Sampler, The Founding Generation*

# Table of Contents

# Table of Contents, continued

# Foreword

Through their ebb and flow, tides create pools along the shore that teem with life. These tide pools add to the beaches' size, beauty, and utility. At the same time, pounding ocean waves endlessly expand or destroy them without mercy.

Great events teem with individuals critical to their outcome. The ocean that is humanity rolls on little noting them. One can say they are the inhabitants of mankind's tide pools. Like the denizens of tide pools, their fates are covered over by the sands of time. *The Tidal Pool* trilogy is about unsung individuals affected by World War II and its aftermath. A majority of participants saw the war as a crusade for freedom. For many others, the war gave them an excuse to perpetrate violence and mayhem. But wars end, and life continues. Escaping from prosecution, many fled to South America to continue their murderous ways for new masters after hostilities ended. Some of their old antagonists were tasked with bringing justice to these same individuals. Their efforts are depicted in this trilogy which spans three continents, four decades, and 11 countries.

The names are changed, but the volumes are based on true events. The initial volume, *Ruler Of The Seas*, must, out of necessity, begin as a love story. Because it is in Caracas that the trilogy's unifying character, Eric Dykman meets and marries a tempestuous Venezuelan heiress. His career is sidetracked when his ship leaves him in Caracas. At the behest of the resident American spy, he becomes an expert at ensuring water-borne war supplies reach the Allies before America's entry into World War II. His efforts are so effective he is made a Nazi assassination target. After America enters the war, his expertise significantly contributes to America's use of ocean highways to claim victory in World War II.

Hence the title, *Ruler Of The Seas*. Significant moral questions are often explored in great novels. While not pretending to put these books on that high shelf, they do contain an ethical dilemma. One such Hobson's choice, deciding whether a murderer lived or died is seldom given to one man alone. Almost never is that decision thrust on him twice. Yet, Eric Dykman was required to render life-or-death judgments twice. In the first incident, he allowed the criminal to live. Years later, he arranged for two evil men to die. The first instance in which he did not act resulted in lifelong regrets. When another such decision was required, he acted differently, with far-reaching consequences.

—Don Mazzella

# Addenda

Nestor In Greek Mythology. King of Pylos, was considered after Ulysses to be the wisest of all Greeks. In the *Iliad*, he often gives advice to the younger warriors and advises Agamemnon and Achilles to reconcile. He is too old to engage in combat himself, but he leads the Pylian troops.

Atelier is a room where artists learn their art, expand their visual acumen, share experiences, exchange ideas, and create their oeuvre.

Condor was the umbrella name for the coordinated German foreign air operations and trade efforts around the world during the Weimar Republic and then under Nazi rule. In South America, among other locales where these activities were particularly strong, the name was used by the airline fostering German nationalism in various Latin countries.

Condor Syndikat was a Brazilian focused German trade company, with headquarters in Berlin and the most successful group founded for trade and spying. Usually, separate entities were set up in each South American country run Germans who became naturalized citizens. Condor Syndikat operated airline services in Brazil while also providing aircraft, maintenance and aviation personnel around the continent. Even opening a route over the Atlantic to Africa. Allied intelligence before the war and during the conflict thought all were heavily used by German spy organizations.

Syndicato Condor obtained the rights and interests of *Condor* Syndikat probably in anticipation of the conflict and prior to World War II. In its original form, Condor Syndikat was partly a subsidiary of Luft Hansa offering passenger and mail services in Brazil. It was renamed Cruzeiro do Sul in 1943. It was also the mother company of the Brazilian airlines Varig and Cruzeiro do Sul.

## "Whoever rules the waves rules the world."

—Alfred T. Mahan

# Characters

**Eric Dykman**: His new wife kept him in Caracas as Naval Attaché. He became a pawn in the pre-war spy efforts by learning methods to improve Allied shipping efforts. Brought to Washington after being marked for death by Nazi spies, he led efforts to move supplies to Europe. His post-war missions are portrayed in volumes two and three.

**Christiana de la Vega Dykman**: The heiress whom every Venezuelan society matron feared their son would marry instead chose the American Navy officer. Able to befriend anyone, her fierce love and dependence changed and enriched her husband's life, but his wartime efforts caused her death.

**Sven Bernadotte**: Able to ply his spy trade before and after World War II in South America. His ruthless tactics enable him to avoid retribution for many years, posing as another man.

**Enrique de la Vega**: Known for his ability to wring added profits from his company by installing operations more efficiently, he loved his daughter but sensed she had a tragic fate.

**Antigone de la Vega**: The wife of Enrique de la Vega, mother to Christiana, reared on an English country estate, she gave Enrique three children and neglected Christiana, but when she was endangered, sheltered her granddaughter.

**Nathan Reed**: Assigned to the American embassy in Caracas as agriculture attaché, he heads espionage operations and recruits Eric Dykman into his world.

**Gertrude Seaman**: Used in her teenage years by the proprietors of an English brothel, she became the successful but violence-prone secret agent banished to South America. Despite this setback, her acumen thwarted agents of three countries.

**Deborah DeCourcy**: An English economist stationed in Caracas, her naiveté led her into danger and ultimate exile in America. Happiness came to her from the most unlikely person.

**Henry Batterson, Earl of Northumberland**: No one did more for Miriam Brinkerman during the war or demanded less. His reward came in the post-war era.

**Flight Lieutenant Ian Harcourt**: In trying to solve problems with his fellow airmen's parachutes during the Battle of Britain, he found Miriam and happiness, if only briefly.

**Miriam Brinkerman Ben-Levin**: A woman at ease with her Zionist father and in the country homes of English aristocracy between wars, she played an essential role in the founding of Israel.

**Admiral Rick Huntington**: Probably Eric's best friend, he learned to love the man's wife and trusted his friend when he asked for help on his final mission.

**Marvel Huntington**: Raised in Tennessee and able to hold her liquor almost as well as Christiana de la Vega, she was the perfect companion to scandalize Washington and advance their husbands' careers.

**Henry J. Kaiser**: The industrial genius who produced thousands of Liberty Ships for the Allies and showed them more efficient industrial production methods. He was Eric's champion in Washington.

**Anthony Massucci**: The boss of the New York docks, his dealings with Eric led to a friendship and, ultimately, Christiana's death.

**Giovanni Perrone**: Hardened to criminal life, this police lieutenant would not rest until he found the perpetrator of a horrible murder.

# January, 1938
## Christiana de la Vega

Desire drove away any other thoughts from men and boys, 13 to 80, just minutes after meeting Christiana de la Vega. Strangers first noted the combination of her English aristocracy skin, black but silken hair, and voluptuous figure.

Then they heard Christiana's soft voice, tinged with an infectious, come-hither tone. Most were quickly drawn into whatever she was doing, often irreverent activities sure to upset someone. Defying the laws of heredity, her green eyes penetrated the innermost secrets of those around her. Thus earning her the title of Green Goddess amongst her contemporaries. Finally, her face wore such a web of concentration, whether talking with a family member or stranger, to create a cone of isolation, excluding others who happened to be nearby.

By agreement of all men in pre-World War II Venezuelan society, her wealth and social position made her that city's most eligible heiress. Yet each of that city's social elite mothers feared the day her son presented Christiana as his betrothed.

Besides her blue blood and beauty, Christiana was the daughter of Enrique de la Vega. Having expanded the family fortune into an international empire, he was one of the most influential businessmen in the country. His marriage evolved unhappily for him. After giving him two sons who were rapidly taking their place as economic and social leaders, his wife chose to live in the wilder reaches of Venezuela, recreating in this foreign land the Cotswold world of her youth.

One son married outside of the traditional Venezuelan ruling families, and the other stayed within the tight circle of the old alliances. Younger by a decade, Christiana was conceived during a brief reconciliation interlude in her parent's estranged marriage.

Growing up, Christiana keenly felt her mother's absence, who lived on her remote ranch while father and daughter made Caracas their home. Seeing this separation's effect on his daughter, the father indulged her excess. But these indulgences did not fill the void in her heart.

Later in the century, psychologists would argue that most of her escapades were attempts to get her mother's attention. Not that she ever lacked other people's attention. Almost from the cradle, Christiana used her looks, intelligence, and infectious manner to draw into her current activity anyone, young or old, related or not, male or female, who was nearby.

Christiana had scandalized Caracas society since her first teen year driving her parents to despair and earning the envy of her social circle. These exploits caused Christiana to be expelled from three schools before employing private tutoring. Three tutors failed to educate her beyond the four languages she spoke and the copious liquor she drank despite her shrewd intelligence.

Despite the claims of intimate friendship by many Caracas society teen girls, Christiana had acquaintances but no confidants. Alone in a big house with an absentee mother and busy father, she developed an insular shell no one had ever cracked. When someone's questions came too close to piercing the shell built around her, Christiana often resorted to sexual ploys or embarked on another of her escapades. One such occurrence involved dressing as a nun to disguise her invasion of the Caracas Bishop's rectory to steal his private wine cache for a party.

Christiana was often described as a devil temptress in a dress during her liquor-soaked evenings with the city's young elites that often ran into the daylight hours. But all her companions agreed they would go to hell to take the garment off. Among the city's wealthy young scions were many suitors willing to risk their mothers' disapproval by wooing the heiress, even in desperation, promising marriage.

She did not overtly reject their advances, always seemingly promising but never delivering as much as they wanted. After a night's flirtations, the would-be Latin lover would anticipate ending the evening in her bedroom, only to find her lifelong nurse sternly blocking the door. In truth, as her teen years drew to a close and other girls already betrothed, despite many attempts, no one had yet pinned her to betrothal or could substantiate the claim she had joined them in bed.

In a society where others settled on a women's husband, society mothers knew Christiana would be the one who chose her husband. Each mother prayed their son would not be the "winner." Given her apparent advantages, wealth, social standing, and beauty, Caracas waited to see who would be the final choice. This was a question her parents separately also asked themselves almost nightly.

Numbered among the wealthiest, most influential men in Venezuela, Christiana's father was accustomed to getting his way. He feared no one or no institution. Over the years, another success followed every success. Sadly, he was sure this would not be the case in Christiana's future. He hoped that there was a possible route to avoiding what he expected would be some fatal event that he knew would be visited on Christiana. He was also confident it would not be of her own making. But he recognized that even he could not change her fate.

The certainty of his forebodings stemmed from events in Christiana's teen years. When she got into trouble, his wealth bought her out of some situations. In others, Christiana's beauty enabled her to escape the consequences of her acts. But he saw some future event to which neither riches nor attractiveness could save her. He thought, in his heart, one or the other would cause the fatal outcome. Calamity, he knew, came even to those that had both beauty and riches. His one hope was perhaps the man she chose would save her? Drawing comfort from that thought made him eager for her to find him. Resigned to having little input into who would be his future son-in-law, he waited for the candidate to appear.

Inside their favorite dress shop, Carlotta Ramirez and Christiana examined frocks for wearing at the coming party thrown by the American ambassador. Bored with their regular suitors amongst Caracas' young blades, they hoped to find some new challenges in the other guests. Unlike Christiana, Carlotta was serious about her studies, hoping to break into her country's male-dominated diplomatic corps. Because her mother died when she was five, she alone shared some of Christiana's feelings of maternal estrangement.

"Another dull party," Carlotta moaned.

"No different, just the same tired people," Christiana said, standing there naked as she usually was when trying on clothes. "I wish I had your figure," Carlotta said, gazing at her friend's form.

"I want your brains," her friend rejoined. "You have them, you just use them for other purposes." "But I have no ambition. You want to be a diplomat. You have a purpose."

"What do you want?" Carlotta asked for the hundredth time.

"If I knew I would tell you."

"You want a man who challenges you."

"Perhaps, I don't know. Certainly not the boys and men we have here."

"Maybe he will float in on the tide or be at tomorrow's party."

"I doubt that," Christiana said, and they both laughed.

# January, 1938
## Eric Dykman

Even in the most urgent situations, drawing a quick solution from Eric Dykman was never possible. Not in his nature were there incentives enough for him to offer glib or incomplete answers. Instead, he would assure himself the solution he was about to give was the best possible in the particular situation facing him. When he was confident of the veracity of his response or suggestion, he would speak up, defending the answer until proven wrong or told as an officer to accept a different solution.

Even in situations demanding rapid response was needed, he systematically reviewed possible alternative answers before vocalizing his thoughts. When he did answer, in most instances, his words were complete, succinct, and invariably the best remedy to the problem. Thus, when obstacles manifested themselves, anyone knowing him soon turned to this quiet boy, teenager, teammate, or companion for the best solution. Through primary grades, at the private school, his widowed mother scrimped to send him, and finally, at the Naval Academy, Eric had the correct answers. It just took him time to get them out of his mouth. Because command at sea requires instantaneous responses to unexpected events, classes at the Naval Academy demanded that midshipmen needed to speak up quickly and accurately when presented with any situation.

Eric's slower responses ensured that he did not always gain the favor of his teachers at the beginning of each semester.

In classes where midshipmen vied to be the first to answer proffered problems, he was not among the first to respond. However, after other students had exhausted the string of possible solutions, instructors at the Academy, where he was the fourth and last generation of his family to attend, learned to wait for Eric's answers, confident of their correctness, accuracy, and completeness. Academy instructors assigned to look for future leaders came to appreciate these qualities. Cognizant of his legacy, they also noted none of his ancestral predecessors retired as Admirals.

Also separating him from others was his intense stare taking in an individual or a room at a glance. To some, including most women, it was a distraction. So, intent on his face, people tended to ignore his six-foot figure and quiet posture of authority. He was not handsome, but some women found him irresistible. He was never without a semi-girl friend, but most relationships ended on the rocks of his quiet certitude, which many young girls could not quite understand or appreciate.

After graduation and even favorable instructor evaluations, this trait did not help his early active-duty career. In his first assignments, naval superiors felt that his stare and delay in answering a question were manifestations of doubt in their decisions. This seeming display of distrust resulted in decidedly negative early evaluations. Through hard work, he overcame any initial negative feelings in all of his assignments, soon becoming a trusted advisor to the commanding officer or captain in every posting.

Naval careers are enhanced or slowed by the nicknames officers earned either at the Academy or shortly after graduation. Another career impediment occurred during an ancient military history course studying the Iliad. A fellow midshipman noticed the similarity in Eric's manner of offering answers to that of the wily Greek, Nestor. After that, his nickname became Nestor, the sly advisor. It followed him throughout his naval career as upon arriving at his next posting, superior officers were wary of their newest officer. After initially fighting the application, he came to accept the nickname and forget the suspicion it engendered.

Eric never looked at himself as a Nestor. But like many things in his life, other people's perceptions of himself were often at odds with his self-evaluation. Nonetheless, others continued to recognize the similarity. The dedicated copy of the Iliad given him by his mother upon his graduation was among his treasured possessions.

Joining the fleet with the depression class of 1931 after graduating eleventh in Academy class ranking, Eric's first seagoing assignment took him to Europe. Before leaving, superiors assigned him an additional task, to review the long-term shipbuilding efforts of key allies and possible enemies. His thorough study of French,

English, and German naval construction and their effect on future conflicts displayed strategic insights informative enough to draw the attention of a group of admirals who were the future supreme naval commanders of World War II.

These officers, like Eric, believed the ability to supply Britain via sea routes would be critical to any Allied victory in Europe. Opening the eyes of other senior officers would take years to wean them from the big gun theories of short wars decided by large fleet-to-fleet engagements. Many older admirals, particularly in the Bureau of Ships and war planning groups, still clung to this doctrine.

Eric and others saw the need for armadas of merchant ships to run the submarine gauntlet they expected in the next war. One person who read his report was Henry J. Kaiser, who tucked it away in his mind along with the officer's name who wrote it. Based on Eric's belief in the future need for large numbers of merchant ships, Kaiser developed the idea of Liberty Ships built quickly and with a cruising speed of eleven knots needed to keep up with convoys.

Also, based on his reports, he spent the next three years in Washington at the Navy department working with senior staff on improving the defenses and deployment of sea-going supply efforts. He became an expert in enhancing the arcane of supply mix, loading, shipboard pre-spotting, and offloading civilian and military cargo. The importance of having this knowledge did not become apparent until war loomed for America. Then, it was the experiences of Britain and her allies that woke Washington leaders to the need for better management of military and civilian ships and cargoes destined for war zones and invasion beaches.

In 1938, these thoughts were far away from Washington Naval leaders. Thinking his views had little impact, Eric gladly left for the routine rotational sea-going appointment critical to advancement as a Lieutenant. This assignment took him to the light cruiser USS Raleigh.

Assigned to the Caribbean fleet, the ship's visit to Caracas, Venezuela, in 1938 changed everything for Eric. Throughout his subsequent life, Eric seldom reflected on his ultimate fate, but when he did, he often wondered what would have been the thread of his life had he not gone to the Embassy party welcoming the ship to Venezuela.

At the time, he was grieving. Before leaving, Eric buried his mother beside his father, who was killed in World War I. With her death, Eric's last ties to his childhood ended. He was always self-contained, studious, and seldom taken to rash, not thought-out acts. He withdrew more into himself on the voyage from Newport, Virginia, to Caracas.

Cajoled by fellow officers to join them in what promised to be a raucous evening following the expected sedate diplomatic affair, he was unprepared for what occurred. In his tropical white uniform,

Standing next to the wall and surveying the guests, Christiana was like an alligator eying the river for potential meals. She attended these affairs in the hopes someone new would attract her attention. The men and boys of Caracas had long since become cookies to be eaten or thrown away once any novelty they possessed bored her. Christiana was adept at attracting any man that caught her attention. None kept it for long. She saw the line of American naval officers as diversions, but none even appealed to her for an evening's entertainment.

As she swept the room, she noted the tall lieutenant who stood somewhat apart from his fellow officers. Unlike them, he looked at both men and women, seemingly shushing out their actual worth in a momentary appraisal. When his face swiveled towards her, she drew inward. He stopped seeing her. Not unusual for men, for there were few more beautiful women in Caracas. But she sensed he was not looking at her body but her soul. No one ever said Christiana shrank from any challenge, appraisal, or unusual man. Unlike her usual response of brazenly returning his stare, she turned away.

Noting his quiet manner and sense of authority and enthralled by the depths of his face and eyes seen from afar as he scanned the room, taking in everything, she weaved her way across the crowded assembly hall to stand in front of him.

Christiana was stunning in her yellow dress wrapped tightly around her body, in high heels, which put her face to his chin. She favored yellows and white because they contrasted with her skin, emerald eyes, and long black hair she always wore tight against her skull in public. It cascaded out to envelop her and whoever was with her when loosened in more private moments.

Knowing her smile's effect on both men and women, she exposed her teeth while grabbing his arm to steer the unsuspecting officer to a side alcove. Christiana bombarded him with questions, not bothering to let him finish his answer before throwing another dart at his mind. All the time, she looked into his eyes, drawing them into the orb of her face.

Eric never remembered what they said, just the overwhelming feeling of helplessness and desire she immediately invoked in him. Knowing her effect on men, Christiana often played the sorceress to the hilt, not the least with her father and brothers.

Christiana babbled meaningless words, allowing her impulses to guide what she said while looking closely into his face. In turn, Eric returned the rapt gaze, unsure what was happening, and both knew they were experiencing something profound and frightening.

Within minutes she took his arm, leading him to a side bathroom. Locking the door, Christiana pulled his pants down and wrapped her legs around his waist. His penis felt the wetness that poured from her. Engorged, it swelled immediately. Surprised by his response, Eric thrust himself inside her with a vigor he had never before credited himself. The suddenness and strength pleased them both. They began a rhythmic pounding against the wall. For a man who measured his every move, pondered every action, this woman elicited something so alien to him it was years before Eric ever really understood, and then only in the arms of another woman.

In the years following, Eric always put aside learning if their first encounter was a new experience for Christiana, nor did he care. For him, those moments in the bathroom were among the most exciting of his life. They never spoke again of that encounter, keeping it a treasured individually never shared memory.

While she was buttoning his trouser after finishing, he heard for the first time the devil-may-care laugh she adapted during the commission of some daring, convention-defying escapade. Opening the door, she ignored the two people waiting in the hall and led him from the embassy. Her chauffeur seemed to have anticipated her early departure as the waiting car was disengaged from the other limousines and ready to roar off. Still spellbound by this vixen, Eric followed not so much meekly as seemingly powerless by the magnetism of their attraction to each other.

Ignoring the traffic around them and the chauffeur in the front seat, they continued to kiss passionately until they reached her house. The pair ran to her room in an oblivious cloud that ignored others.

They made love in a delirium of moods never felt before and detached from any of Eric's experiences through the night and into the following day. Despite all the self-control instilled in him almost from birth, he surrendered to the woman utterly, whose spontaneous hugging drove all other thoughts from him.

# May, 1938
## Christiana de la Vega

Midway through this first period of knowing each other, Eric realized how much liquor his partner drank. Knowing his mother drank herself almost to death, he gently admonished her swilling. Fiercely throwing her half-full glass at his, she moved to pour another from the bottle next to the bed, and Eric moved swiftly and grabbed it from her hand.

"You can have the bottle or me, but not both," he said to her in a low, firm voice.

"You would give me up for drinking?" she asked in surprise, for no one had said these words before to her.

"That is the choice you must make, and make it now. If you choose that bottle, I am out of here.

"And you would give up this body?" She said, uncovering herself, sure she could change his mind."

"Yes, because I know what drink can do to a woman."

"But not to a man?"

"To a man as well. But we are talking about a lifetime together."

"So, you think this is not a fling, and you go back to your ship?

"You think I am a fool? You can leave any man, but no man could ever leave you. But this is one man who will leave this moment if you drink another drop,"

"You really would leave me? Leave this? You want me to believe that?"

"Yes. This moment. This time. Forever. I know it would be hard for me to leave now, but we are doomed if you continue to drink in excess."

"Then I stop now. Not totally, but always when you are near and most times when you're not."

"Then I stay."

Totally entranced with each other, they did not care what others were thinking. But many people were thinking of them. Having seen their rapid departure, his shipmates covered for him at the embassy and on the *Raleigh*. Pleased, his voyage-long funk was about to end but jealous of the prize he had won.

Coming home to be greeted by a gaggle of hovering servants, Christiana's father, Enrique de la Vega, began pounding uselessly on the door. Only his English-born wife's counsel prevented him from breaking down the door. Antigone de la Vega was estranged from her husband but shared his fear for their daughter's fate. Antigone only attended the Embassy party to keep her eyes on the rebellious daughter she secretly envied. Watching the initial encounter between daughter and naval officer, she saw a glimmer of hope in the man's obvious challenge to her inner strength. Grumbling, the father accented to her wishes. Together, the estranged parents waited.

Never abandoning the bed except for brief interludes of food smuggled in by her Duennas, Christiana and Eric discovered the others' bodies in ways neither had known existed. In his instance, because of lack of prior interest and, in her case, lack of years.

After parting at her door to the relief of all other house occupants, exhausted but at peace with himself, he was ready for the deserved shipboard punishment awaiting him. While Eric was onboarding his ship, Christiana ignored her father's anger to see the lieutenant again. When the father threatened retribution against the American, she countered his threats by disclosing plans to run away if he pressed charges.

Fearing a public scandal, Christiana's father communicated his anger towards the naval officer to the American ambassador and eventually *Raleigh's* captain. At first, he expressed angry demands aimed at the officer. What the father ultimately wanted, the two Americans were unsure. Neither did he, but because Christiana was displaying the repertoire of moods she had successfully used in the past to get her way, he finally agreed to the American's visits. As the romance continued and she continued to want this American lieutenant beyond the usual period of her dalliances, the father saw the changes he was making in his daughter. Not the least in the daughter's drinking habits. When the visitor was around, there was no drinking.

Unable to withstand Christiana's wailings and despited the young officer being almost 13 years his daughter's senior, the father prevailed on the ambassador to encourage *Raleigh's* captain to permit the young officer unlimited shore leave. This obviously did not sit well with his fellow officers, whose initial good-natured complicity to his escapade turned to jealousy and hostility.

Unconcerned with their feelings and totally mesmerized by the girl-woman, Eric became a willing companion to her youthful madness. Much to Eric's surprise, his passion for one of the most beautiful women in the city did not abate. Instead, it grew each time he saw her, and his lust showed more vital each moment they tussled in her bed.

Knowing one of them needed to keep a sense of perspective, Eric sought to balance their romps with efforts to learn more about Christiana. To do this required him to reject some of her blandishments. Growing up, Christiana had little contact with her mother, and her father's indulgences did not fill the void in her heart. Most of her escapades were attempts at getting her mother's attention. Add her looks, intelligence, and ability to draw in anyone eight to eighty, and you had a woman with many acquaintances but no true friends. When one of his questions came too close to piercing the shell she had built, Christiana resorted to her sexual ploys.

Knowing how important it was for them to build a relationship beyond sex, Eric tried to control his emotions and feelings. For Eric, this was a constant battle that he sometimes lost. In truth, Christiana's smile and provocative touches aroused Eric never experienced the passions she brought out. Nor was he totally comfortable with some of her habits or approaches to everyday encounters. Clearly, she was entirely too friendly with strangers, particularly men. Her approach to sociability led many men to take as invitations to romance. This concern he soon found was shared with her father.

In the end, weighing everything, he realized he could not ever leave her. Finally, he resigned himself to accepting Christiana for what she was and knowing he had found one of life's rare magnetic forces. Admitting to himself, he was happier than he had ever been.

Sensing a chance to influence this Venezuelan business elite, the American ambassador prevailed on the captain to relieve Eric of his shipboard duties. All assumed these special privileges would be in place while the ship was in port. Again, the "luck" Nestor was enjoying was not pleasing to other officers who needed to take up his duties for him. For the first time in his memory, Eric didn't care. Seeing Christiana was the main focus of his mind. Put aside were any thoughts of what would happen when his ship left.

In pre-war Caracas, the ambassador was a wily veteran assigned to the Venezuelan capital because he dared to argue against State Department leaders' relationship vis-a-vis Hitler. After reading Eric's file was shrewd enough to decide the officer could be helpful in the spy wars raging across the continent. In particular, his talents involving trade and seaborne transit could prove beneficial. Even if others in Washington hadn't realized it yet, the ambassador knew America would need the foods, ores, and oil locked in South America in any coming conflict.

Like the British and French, some officials in America viewed South American resources as critical to supplying foodstuffs, ores, and other materials if war should break out in Europe. A wily old diplomat, the ambassador always sought the advantages needed to carry out his duties. Suddenly Eric was here, a valuable new pawn in the run-up to war which he was sure was coming. Already, he was proving helpful in creating favorable relations with Enrique de la Vega. Eric could also prove vital in keeping goods flowing to America and its allies. It was an asset not to be wasted.

In Venezuela, Christiana's father was known as a man to get things done privately or within the government. Demanding pieces of those enterprises he helped had made Enrique de la Vega an immensely wealthy man. He was also an astute manager of his wealth. Partnering with First National City Bank's country head, he moved significant funds to the United States.

Unusual for a Latino father, and despite her foibles, Christiana was his favorite child. For this reason, half of his American holdings were held in trust until her 25th birthday. Now, with an American husband, his decision proved prophetic. Sadly, also, he knew his daughter and whatever children she might have would at some time move to the United States.

In the future, what was happening now with this American gave him hope. The envy and jealousy of his fellow officers continued as

Eric was granted detached leave to stay in the city, letting him spend almost every day and night at the de la Vega home, rather too grand to be called a simple casa.

With a fatherly warning, the ambassador gently suggested Eric try to make amends with Christiana's father. While both men were naturally reticent, Eric nonetheless made it a point to talk with him at every opportunity. Unexpectedly, their talks bore fruit, blossoming into a warm friendship.

During this courting time and over the years, Christiana's father and Eric discovered mutual interests besides the girl-woman they both loved. While still relatively young, Enrique had been forced to take control of the family businesses, originally cattle raising and meatpacking. Under him, it was greatly expanded through the father's unique ability to analyze how things worked and find ways to make them operate smoother and more profitably. As the family fortune grew, so did the father's reputation. In envy and, some in jealousy, Christiana's father was known as the Tinkerer, which translates to *El Manipulator* in Spanish.

Getting to know the man infatuated with his daughter, the father soon realized Eric was also an accomplished tinkerer. Like the older man, the suitor reveled in finding more efficient ways of accomplishing any task or series of operations. Because he always sought more efficient ways to do the same things his competitors did, enabled *El Manipulador's* enterprises to enjoy greater profits. Once Enrique understood Eric's knack for easing naval tasks, their talks and idea exchanges became lengthy, sometimes to Christiana's frustration. This common bond soon drew the men into a life-long friendship far beyond mere filial bonds.

Enrique separated his holdings because neither of Christiana's two brothers, heirs to the family's Venezuelan fortune, shared their father's interest in understanding how fundamental finding ways of doing things more efficiently was to be successful businessmen. Much of the father's disappointment and sadness lay in their neglect to find added roads to efficiency. He knew. As they did not, making things work better drove continued success that added profits and the reward. As caretakers instead of innovators, he was confident in their abilities to sustain his legacy, but that was all he expected of them.

With the *Raleigh* scheduled to depart, the father approached the ambassador again. Quick consultation among the Ambassador, Naval Department, and the State Department resulted in the ship departing with one less officer. There was a new naval attaché in Caracas and one the ambassador knew would be more than an ornament in coming months.

The change at the American embassy and in Christiana did not escape Caracas society, nor foreign emigres who spotted the couple at local social events and entertainment venues. What everyone noted was the besotted way the couple looked at each other. There was one other change undeniable in Christiana's behavior. Prior to meeting the American, she was a hard-drinking, flighty, whimsical, light-hearted force of nature in the young rich set of Caracas society. In the hothouse of elite pre-war Venezuela, it was the stuff of legend. With her new beau, Christiana's drinking had almost totally stopped. Whenever in public, she limited herself to one martini. The change was greeted with much sadness in some circles.

Gone too were the days when she flirted and beguiled any man who came into her orbit. Since her early teens, she left many young, eligible Venezuelans feeling frustrated at the end of many an evening with her. Now, oblivious to all others, she had eyes only for the officer, who remained enthralled with her.

Given the heat of their flirtations, no one was surprised when the invitations announced the engagement and soon-to-be wedding of the Venezuelan heiress and American naval officer.

All the while, Eric was swept along by emotions he had never experienced before. For one, Christiana was insatiable in her sexual demands and displayed multiple mercurial moods. Swinging from highs of enthusiasm for the ceremony to the lows of depression, she worried about little things but neglected such more significant matters as where they would live. Most frustrating was the weight she seemed to be gaining. Discreetly, her *Duenas* brought in a doctor who confirmed what Christiana feared. Unsure of Eric's reaction, she shrieked out the news announcing her pregnancy to him as they lay astride her bed less than 10 days from their wedding.

Gulping in surprise but secretly pleased, he waited for her true feelings to show. Her face displayed anger at the cruel event, making her a mother before she was a wife. Calming her, Eric suggested they tell her father. At this point, she sprang from the bed to grab a nearby statue and hurled it at him.

"Never, it would hurt him too much." She spat.

"I doubt that. I think your father would be pleased."

"Promise you will not tell."

"If you wish, but he can count."

"We will have two weeks for what you call a honeymoon. There I will have an abortion. I am too young to be a mother."

It was Eric's turn to get angry.

"We will have this baby, and we will love it. Afterwards you can swank around all you want, but this baby will happen."

Christiana heard the iron in Eric's voice and pouted. In this instance, she was willing to betray her religion but obeyed him.

"What about your mother?"

"She probably knows already. My cow of a Duenas would have told her as soon as she knew."

"Is that bad?"

"Yes, she thinks I will settle down and be a good wife."

"Never happen with you. I need to take you as you are."

"Do you mean that?"

"Of course. You can change a little but not totally. You will always be you."

"And you accept that?

"It is why I love you."

"Good, let's make love now before I grow fat as a cow."

Their first conversation about her drinking gave her insight into the other side of Eric, his strength of character. Something she needed to balance her own failings. Shocked at the intensity of her initial feelings for Eric, if ever she thought of ending their affair disappeared when she realized what it would mean to her. While she may have been the initial aggressor in the relationship, on many things, in any contest of wills, Eric was a rock against whom her wiles could not move. To her pleasure, this reassured Christiana she had made the right choice. It was one of the reasons she loved him even more fiercely each day they were together.

Realizing her mercurial nature, Christiana needed to marry a man able to withstand her blandishments and wiles. She also understood her addiction to liquor. In Eric, she recognized the man who would deal with both. Despite his early surrender, his firm will often come through either when they were alone or with people. In all things, beyond a certain point, he would not go or let her venture. This was something somehow known to her from the first moment she gazed across the room.

Christiana realized she needed someone like Eric to give her strength to quell her inner demons, of which alcohol was one. Often, she regretted the impulsive acts she committed and whose actions troubled others. Many happened after drinking too much. Realizing her helplessness in preventing them, they bothered her as well. They represented walls she needed to climb or destroy, whether it had to do with men, authority, or convention. In particular, and for reasons she did not understand, men were like chocolate. She craved them, but they were of little use once tasted or suckled.

While young, Christiana developed a sure instinct when it came to men. Almost from the cradle, she sensed their strengths and weaknesses. Her father, *EL Manipulador*, was her first conquest. Her brothers were the second and third. But she knew in Eric she had the man she needed. Control her no, no one could do that. But one who would always be there to protect her. For Christiana recognized that left to herself, she was doomed to destroy anyone or anything she touched.

In the beginning, she toyed with the idea this would be another fling. But Eric was made of different cloth, and she realized he was the best possible marital match for her. If it meant having the baby, it would be the price she would pay for the man she would come to love completely.

His rock was the foundation she needed to build a life. The baby was their first test, and Eric proved equal to the challenge.

# June, 1938
## Christiana de la Vega Dykman

All of Venezuelan society turned out for the wedding. Held on the grounds of *El Manipulator*'s estate, Christiana barely fit in her wedding gown, avoiding the knowing looks of her bridesmaids. The American ambassador acted as best man, and the lineup to greet the new couple lasted more than an hour.

At the reception afterward, Eric met many people for the first time, his ship had sailed without him, and he was grateful for the Embassy group who attended.

Midway through the night, a man who worked for the Rockefeller farming imitative walked up and introduced himself.

"Congratulations. Great wedding. Great feed." He said.

"You are?" Eric asked, unsure of the man.

"Nathan Reed, I work with the Rockefeller foundation on agricultural improvement."

"Glad you could come. Nice to have some fellow Americans."

"Glad to be here. Wonder if you could do me a favor when you get back from your honeymoon?"

"Ah, what."

"Wonder if you can look at export records along the coast from Venezuela south."

"And that interests you why?"

"Want to know what are the best crops to plant here and further south from an expert's point of view."

Suddenly, Eric's mind drifted back to a brief conversation with the ambassador. The veteran diplomat hinted cryptically Eric's job was more than entertaining an heiress. "You may be asked to look at some naval issues from people in the field," was the ambassador's directive. "Do it."

Peering intently at the man, he thought their conversation was light-hearted banter realizing there and then that he did more than offer advice to farmers.

"Be happy to," Eric said pleasantly.

"Figured you would. Nice party and I hope you enjoy your honeymoon."

Hardly had the first man strolled away than another stranger approached. In a room of white-suited Latinos he stood out with blond hair, blue eyes, white skin, and dark clothes.

"Allow me to congratulate you, Commander Eric, you have married the most interesting woman in Caracas.

"An unusual way of describing my wife," Eric replied, calling Christiana, his wife for the first time, and to a stranger.

"Only because she has bewitched so many men and drawn the fear of so many mothers."

"How so?" replied Eric, miffed by the intimacy of the man's comments but intrigued by the statement.

"First an introduction, I am Sven Bernadotte, special assistant to the head of Luft Hansa here in South America."

"Ah, a man of influence. Now I know why you're here but not your comment."

"Because they feared their sons would bring her home as a bride and she has led astray many of their daughters."

"Hardly a pleasant thing to say to a husband on first meeting and at his wedding."

"My apologies, for I envy you. You have married into a lifetime of adventure.'

"I thought all marriages were adventures."

"Yes, but yours will be more adventurous than most. When you return to Caracas, I hope we may dine together at lunch. I work with Luft Hansa and we should get to know each other."

"I look forward to it," Eric replied, moving away from the man without knowing why but sensing there was more to the invitation that met the eye.

As Eric made his way across the room, the ambassador intercepted him.

"I see you speaking to our resident agent."

"The Swede?"

"No he's a kraut pretending to be Swedish, no our agricultural expert who doesn't know corn from alfalfa unless it is labeled. Do what he asks and keep me informed about the other one if you do meet again."

Eric laughed to himself as he made his way toward Christiana.

"Now I am in the spy game," not realizing how prophetic the thought was.

Christiana's face revealed how tired and flush the day had been. She welcomed his appearance. Looking at her, Eric again felt the surge of warmth so new to him. Her kiss held promise as she kissed him on the lips; they sought out her parents and left shortly afterward. The party itself lasted three days, but no one missed them.

Christiana spent most of the honeymoon at her mother's ranch in the bathroom with morning sickness that lasted most of the day.

Their return to the city occurred with the simultaneous disclosure of impending motherhood to her family. Ensconced in a villa halfway between the embassy and her parent's home, Christiana endured a very difficult pregnancy leaving her forever fearful of a second child. Alexandra Dykman was born on the same day Sven Bernadotte received orders from Dresden to begin activating a particular group for the Spymaster. It was the first of many coincidences twixt Eric Dykman and the killer, Sven Bernadotte.

# January, 1939
## Nathan Reed

Caracas business and society recovered slowly from the holiday festivities, which only ended with the last celebrations on Three Kings Day. The months after the wedding was difficult for Christiana. Her figure disappeared and with it her sense of humor or good manners. In their place were periods of moodiness, anger, and foreboding. She took it out on all those around her, especially Eric. Finally, on his father-in-law's advice, he sent for her mother.

With her arrival, there was a change in Christiana. Christiana became the docile child of a strong but solicitous mother. Her presence was needed as complications in the pregnancy worried the doctors. Throughout the final months of Christiana's confinement, they were concerned.

Christiana and everyone else left things in her mother's hands, and four days after the New Year, the result was there in the cradle for all to behold, especially Eric.

The birth of his daughter found Eric strangely happy, knowing mother and child were well. Christiana had banished him from her bed four months into her confinement. Now, he could hear her exercising and see her dieting trying to regain the figure which was her pride. He also noted that liquor was no longer in her daily regimen except for the Champagne drunk celebrating the birth. Something her parents saw as well.

With the embassy short-staffed, Eric was pressed into service as a senior member. It was a task he rather enjoyed learning the workings of an arcane institution that served as an outpost for his country. Often, Eric would find Nathan Reed sitting alone in his office. Since his wedding and remembering the Ambassador's words, he had become friends with the thin man who rarely spoke about his work. The two men had taken to leave the embassy during the traditional siesta hours and sit at the small outdoor café across the square that fronted the embassy.

On the last Wednesday in January, they were there when Sven Bernadotte ambled by as if out on a stroll.

"Well the cat is out of the bag now," Reed said.

"Meaning?"

"You know who Bernadotte is?"

"He works for the German air group."

"That's his cover, he runs German spies here on the continent."

"Then what was all that all about?"

"He as telling me he knew what I really did."

"So it is true, you do more that help farmers?"

"Yes, but more importantly, he's telling you to stay out of the game."

"A little late isn't it?"

"Yes I guess so. Now you need to be extra careful."

"I don't know how else to be."

The two men sat back and drank the last of their drinks before returning to the embassy.

# September, 1939
## Sven Bernadotte

Given his name, when asked about his relationship to the Royal houses of Sweden, Sven Bernadotte always deflected them in such a manner as to suggest either some nefarious act or illegitimacy estranged him to exile to South America. A continent settled by emigres, either background gave him an air of mystery that prevented further questions, and this suited him.

Claiming to be Swedish, he spoke that language and Spanish with a Teutonic accent reflecting his early German schooling. His Swedish was flawless, his Spanish less so, and he pretended not to be well versed in German. In his three-year career working for Luft Hansa, he was tested in all three, and the general staff consensus was that he best be avoided, which also suited him.

The way he carried out any assignment and his ability to swoop in to accomplish tasks earned him a particular name——the Condor. A code name that lasted a lifetime.

Arriving from Berlin via Stockholm in 1936, he was positioned as an advisor to Luft Hansa's managing director. His boss was instructed to hire him from a particular unit outside Berlin and not controlled by the Army's secret service, the Abwehr, and then told to leave him alone. After meeting him for the first time, the manager was only too happy to obey those orders. Both men took an instant dislike to the other. For Bernadotte, being ignored as much as possible permitted him the freedom he needed for his mission.

As per his orders, Bernadotte focused his efforts on ensuring foodstuffs, metals, and textiles reaching Germany in peacetime continued at the same or higher levels during any future conflict. That conflict, everyone was confident, was near at hand. Bernadotte became an expert in trade matters across the continent to accomplish this mission. Focusing on the critical elements of international trade, the people dispatching the cargoes, and those who actually labored on moving those goods, he became a familiar figure on the docks and mercantile centers throughout the continent.

Bernadotte had few scruples and quickly learned who to bribe on the docks, where pressure was needed to force government officials to clear targets, and who to hire if more robust tactics were required. He wasn't above getting his hands dirty in these matters. Where knife, club, or gun was needed, Bernadotte helped people favorably inclined toward Germany end up in control of the docks and railroads. On the western side of the continent, Bernadotte felt comfortable supplies to Germany would continue to move towards Europe.

With his mixture of languages, the air of authority, and a willingness to do anything necessary, Bernadotte built up a vast network of individuals to accomplish any task. His main objective remained to ensure the smooth passage of goods to Germany. He also created phantom companies with ties to Spain and Sweden. Each country was expected to be neutral in any coming conflict. Both countries were sympatric to German interests. One, Spain, willingly, and the other, Sweden, desirous of being free and unoccupied from the surrounding German tide.

Busy as he was and despite his efforts to hide his activities, Bernadotte's machinations did not escape British intelligence, mainly regarding important ores such as tin, copper, and iron. Considering South America as their backyard, the Americans as well perked up when Bernadotte appeared in cities like Buenos Aires and Lima.

Both Allied and German leaders recognized the vital role South American countries would play in any conflict. Keeping ships moving safely through the oceans would require people on the ground in every port and critical rail junction. Roads were almost non-existent in the southern hemisphere, so the railroads were essential to getting any materials to the docks. In those transshipping areas, the yard crews, stevedores, and seamen needed to be the prime targets for disruption and corruption.

Bernadotte's mission was to establish favorable feelings towards Germany's efforts with all groups. Where bribery and flattery didn't work, he was encouraged to use force to ensure those sympathetic to the Nazi goals led the unions and companies.

Starting almost from the first day he arrived, Bernadotte employed all three methods to gain footholds from Caracas to Buenos Aries. He was suspected by Allied intelligence of at least four murders and assorted mayhem. But he was better, however, at cajoling, and his superiors in Germany were happy as he met Eric on his wedding day.

Concerned only with building up his airline and wary of his new assistant, the manager kept most operational details close to his vest. Bernadotte, for his part, wanted little to do with the everyday operations of what was the biggest, most efficient air carrier in South America. From the start, his role was to build up a network of agents across the continent and have them ready for whatever conflict his masters in Berlin thought would happen.

Bernadotte knew his string of agents was outside the Abwehr led by Admiral Wilhelm Franz *Canaris,* who ruled his operatives with an iron fist.

He preferred his lone-wolf operation because he felt his whole life was one of being alone. His allegiance was to the group in Dresden, which was often in conflict with Canaris. Ironically, by not reporting to Canaris, he escaped any retribution for many years of the post-war punishment of Nazi spies.

Born in Berlin two years into the 20th Century, his mother was a renowned actress, and his father was a member of the German General Staff. Happy in his home life, Bernadotte was shattered in 1911 when his mother suddenly took him from his first school and boarded an afternoon train to Stockholm. In the glare of publicity, she left his father for a Swedish royal family member. As an aspiring producer, his future step-father met Bernadotte's mother and abandoned his family to be with her. The couple decided to live in Stockholm because his two children resided there. Brazenly accepting the stares of his social circle, they soon found a place in society. Taking her six-year-old child was almost an afterthought.

The coming years were not kind to her child, who was renamed Sven and given the Bernadotte surname. Unhappy in his new home, he was shuffled from Swedish school to Swedish school. Never accepted either away at school or home with his step-siblings, he came to hate his mother. She dealt with his hatred by blocking him out of her life. Finally, at the age of 13, he was sent back to his father.

Stung by his wife's action and unable to face the disgrace, his father took to drinking and disliked his son from the moment he returned. Despite wartime vacancies, the father never achieved high rank and died in the last month of World War I in a futile charge on the Western front.

Before the war, Bernadotte was shuffled off to a military school. Taunted by fellow students because of his German intermingled with Swedish accent and words, Bernadotte nonetheless excelled as a cadet. Failing to ingratiate himself with his fellow students, he was never elected a cadet leader.

Seeking action but held back to train as officers, his class was slated for induction in January 1919. They were put forward to the summer of 1918 to prepare for the massive German offensive designed to win the war before the Americans could add to the Allied strength.

To Bernadotte's surprise, no German regiment offered him a commission equal to what every other cadet received. Instead, he went to France as a non-commission officer. He proved fearless, heedless of danger, and careless with his men's lives.

Commissioned in the field, he rose to the equivalent of a major and survived the war unscathed. Interestingly, none of his officers or men said goodbye at the German border railroad station when the unit disbanded at war's end.

Adrift, he made his way to Stockholm, demanding rather than pleading with his mother to find him a position. Her husband arranged to send Bernadotte to Paraguay to represent a Swedish steel company. He was anxious to rid the household's painful memory,

Employing the same ruthless tactics learned in wartime, Bernadotte became the top representative in South America within two years. Along the way, he managed to antagonize all the company officials on the continent and in Sweden.

Sensing his days with the Swedish company were numbered, he switched to a German company taking many accounts with him. As the decade turned, Bernadotte found himself in Caracas in the week Germany sent its giant dirigible *Hindenburg* to demonstrate transatlantic service. German war veterans living in the city were offered rides on the giant airship.

The trip exhilarated him, and he was reluctant to disembark. At the airway, an official stopped him with an invitation for drinks. Despite the civilian clothes, the man was obviously a high-ranking officer. By how others in the party and crew treated him, Bernadotte saw his companion enjoyed great authority.

They switched to German at the gentleman's hotel.

"Are you glad to be down on the ground?" the man said, sitting in the hotel bar area.

"I enjoy a plane ride, but that bag of gas makes me proud to be a German."

"I am glad to hear you hold Germany is such esteem. Heil!"

"Heil! Bernadotte said reluctantly, not wanting to be too public with his feeling knowing they would hurt his sales should it get brooded about.

"Nonetheless, one spark and poof it is over."

"It does demonstrate we are coming back from the war."

"The Hindenburg is just the start."

"Yes, just the start."

"Are you enjoying your stay in South America?" The man's tone shifted from light banter to serious undertones not lost on Bernadotte.

"When I do not need to work with these peasants."

"You seem to do well with their leaders."

"Most see me as a meal ticket."

"Does that bother you."

"Yes and no. Yes, because I want so much more and no because they are the people who will allow me to get what I want."

"And what do you want?"

"Money, power, a company of my own. Even a pretty woman."

"There are enough women here for any man."

"But watch out for their fathers. The father can have a mistress but the daughter must be a wife first."

"An age-old problem."

"It is harder here. The women watch other women."

"Still, you manage to find a way, don't you, Herr Volken."

Bernadotte was shaken hearing his childhood name spoken so casually in a bar halfway around the world. All his senses came awake as he soon realized this was suddenly no longer a casual conversation but something much more.

"I see I have your attention," the older man spoke lower as he edged closer.

"More than my attention."

"Good, I have come a long way to speak with you and with little time to do so."

"What is it you wish to speak?"

"As the English say, of cabbages and kings."

Unsure as to how to reply, Bernadotte remained silent. A nearby clock clicked by two minutes while the two men sat silently. Their waitress walked past them, saw the drinks were untouched, and continued to the following table. Overhead, fans whiffed dry smoke-filled air past them, each waiting for the other to talk.

Finally, the older man broke their silence, drawing from his breast pocket the battered notebook he jotted essential musings in a code only he understood.

"Mustered Major with no pension; a nasty co-worker who is only tolerated because of success selling; Swedish national but German by birth. I could give you more, but these are the essential facts.

"They wouldn't dare fire me."

"They would if they could. You do not deal well with others."

"You are here to tell me this?"

"No, I am here to offer you a new career."

"Why should I want a new career?"

"Because your current career has a top and you have reached it."

"Says, you."

"You know I am right. You can find another company. Another sector, but always a salesman. I have something more in mind for you."

"And how do you know so much about me,"

"I knew your father. Know what happened to him. Know your life. Know how to make you happy and very well paid. Not rich but with, what shall I say are benefits."

"Possibly, but who are you."

"Who I am is nothing. What I represent is everything. There is a new order coming and you can be part of it."

"Do you mean this Nazi order? Adolf Hitler is a flash. To be swept away in the next election."

"If you believe that, you are a fool. But do not think about what he stands for but what it will mean for ambitious men like you."

"You really believe in this shit."

"Yes, and you should to. Not for what they believe but what you can make for yourself in the coming years. Choose the right side and your life is made."

"And you have chosen?"

"I am here now and reaching out my hand to you."

Bernadotte was not a fool and sensed in this man his chance to be bigger than he ever dreamed. Huddling into the night, the men made a pact. Bernadotte would return to Germany for training in Dresden. After some time, he would relocate to South America and work for the National Socialists.

With much trepidation about the future but loving the voyage, he left on the Hindenburg's return voyage, replacing his mentor on the passenger list. With other business needed to be consummated, the latter preferred to return later by boat. In an ironic post-script, Bernadotte's recruiter died in Hindenberg's airborne disaster above the skies in New Jersey years later. He was rushing to America to finalize the details of a new spy ring that existed into the war years.

Bernadotte disappeared into a depressed Germany, spending the next three years learning spycraft and conducting missions across Europe. During this time, he killed three men and one woman on orders from the man whose only title was Spymaster.

# December, 1940
## Eric Dykman

Eric crisscrossed the continent absorbing large drafts of information on shipping and dockage involving Atlantic coast countries from Venezuela to Paraguay and on the Pacific Side, Chile, during baby Alexandra's first years. In the beginning, Eric was learning as much as he could about port facilities; shipping habits; vessel procurement; manifests, customs, and trade financing.

Soon, Eric began to see ways of improving how tasks could be done better. Critical to this process was his need to improve his Spanish and Portuguese. Soon, he progressed to the point they were almost second nature for him to use at home and in commerce. This fluency was not lost on his wife, father-in-law, or Embassy staff.

When talking to Alexandra, he insisted on conversing in English, encouraging her to be totally bilingual. Fluent in two languages when she arrived in Washington as a toddler, she added French in high school and German in college.

The inevitable war came to Europe in September 1939. Seeking to stay neutral, countries in South America tried to balance their relations with the belligerents. As everyone expected, the continent proved an important source of beef, metals, cloth, horses, and other critical war supplies. These countries initially sold to both sides.

Different problems faced both sides in the opening months of the war. Having purchased war goods, foodstuffs, and raw materials, Germany and England needed to move them from South America to the European continent. Each had a different set of problems.

Its superior naval strength enabled England to stifle much of Germany's South American trade within six months of the war's beginning. To keep supplies coming to Germany, agents turned to neutral countries, notably Sweden and Spain. Together with South American flagged vessels and disguised merchantmen, it sought to maintain import levels at pre-war levels.

Due mainly to his efforts, those warships could not totally contain Bernadotte's continued dispatching of vital supplies from the Eastern continental countries. For most of 1940 and 1941, supplies were sent to Germany in Spanish and Swedish flagged ships loaded by sympathetic stevedores and passed through any government controls under the eyes of carefully suborned night watchmen.

Primed by secret agents on both sides, a violent, continent-wide secret war was waged, eventually drawing in Eric. Allies and Axis powers knew the oceanic supply lines were essential factors needed to win the war. Eric considered the conflict in South America to be a prelude to America's struggles when it joined the contest.

Against the Allies, German U boats, surface raiders, and pocket battleships proved to be menaces to ships bringing these vital supplies to Great Britain. German sympathizers existed in almost every country and used covert and subtle means to disrupt the ocean-borne flow. No ship sailed without German intelligence knowing about it, much to the credit of Bernadotte. He also sought and often succeeded in identifying or copying routing orders issued to ships. Again, working through German embassies, he was able to vector submarines towards likely rendezvous locations or chokepoints in the South Atlantic.

Not content in this role, he also sought ways of sabotaging ships, cargoes, and communications. To this, Bernadotte sometimes resorted to murder and extortion. How he did this was not identified until after the war and made him a wanted war crimes criminal.

Eric was not surprised to find Reed, his wedding reception conferee, deeply involved in this cauldron of conspiracies. Not wanting to get sucked into these intrigues, Eric avoided him as much as possible whenever his appearances at the embassy brought him close. This worked until his Ambassador told him bluntly to help. Their first conversation was awkward.

"I need you to look at ways of speeding loading in Paraguay," was Reed's opening gambit.

"What makes you think I can do anything?"

"Because you did it earlier this year in Maracaibo."

"That easy. They just needed more training and less paperwork."

"I think it is more leadership and less slackness in Paraguay."

"Why will the port officials listen to me?"

"You saved them a lot of money last time and those Padrones only understand money in their pockets."

"It's a long trip on lousy railroads."

"Plane is at the airport now, be there in two days and it will wait for you to return."

"I'll try."

"Don't try, do." Reed's voice had none of the softness expected of an agricultural expert.

Eric left that night with a single change of clothes, returning 10 days later with a terse report. "It's done but no one but the bosses are happy."

"Knew you would succeed," Reed said.

"It's what I like to do."

"I'll have more work for you in the future."

"I don't work for you."

"You do now."

He was secretly pleased he solved the problems. Eric chewed on Reed's words during the next two days. He had no conclusions when he returned to the embassy after a day with Alexandra.

With those few words, Reed thanked him and waited just a few days to throw another bottleneck at him, this time off Brazil's coast. Involving convoy coordination, the problem demonstrated to Eric how officials' regarded Reed's active collusion with the British Navy. He wondered if Reed's Washington superiors knew the extent of his involvement. All the Ambassador would say was he should continue helping Reed. His query in code to naval headquarters was ignored but not overlooked.

By the fall of 1940, at Reed's behest, Eric talked directly with British counterparts across South America, anticipating German attack points, rerouting convoys, and hiding critical war material shipments amongst American bottoms or other neutral ships.

A pleasant one for Reed and his British counterparts, the naval officer's knowledge and acumen in ship loading, dispatching and routing proved especially valuable. British officials soon came to utilize his talents in assembling convoys and sending them in ways to thwart U boats lurking off the South American coast. Eric soon realized the most danger existed for these ships when they approached the European and African shores.

Eric pointed this out and offered his radical solution to his English counterparts. In his analysis, the British spread their anti-submarine units too far into the Atlantic, and they sent anti-u-boat ships as far as the South American coasts. Eric persuaded the British liaisons to move their anti-submarine units closer to the European continent based on his observations. He also argued, u boats would find it harder to intercept lone ships if they were dispatched covertly from South American ports on an irregular basis.

Under Eric's plan, ships leaving South American ports were spaced so that the slower ships went first and the faster vessels days later. The faster vessels would catch up with the slower ships as they neared Europe. Forming together as a convoy, scarce patrol units would then join to protect them. As Eric had pointed out in his pre-war summary, any convoy was only as fast as its slowest ship. With limited patrol vessels protecting the newly formed convoy near Europe, they could effectively double their effectiveness until additional units were available.

Beneficial to Britain was Eric's advice on loading ships so they could be more efficiently unloaded at crowded English piers. This knowledge became imperative when America entered the war.

During their time together, despite what his cover employment might say, Eric realized Reed was a key figure in American spy efforts in South America. The spy went around the continent without an armed escort and, seemingly invulnerable to reprisals, worried him.

Following Naval command stricture to remain neutral, Eric was clearly sympathetic to the Allied efforts. Under Reed's gentle prodding, he turned his considerable talents to speeding up Allied supply efforts.

Still viewing it more as a game, his shock came when Reed was killed along with three British naval officers in a Lima apartment. They were at a meeting Eric had planned to attend, but Alexandra's high fever caused him to miss it.

Worried the close call portended other attempts on his life, after conferring with the Ambassador and after signals with Washington unbeknown to Eric centered on his importance within days, Eric was ordered to Washington without delay.

Before he left Caracas via cable, he was asked to prepare a report on Western Hemisphere trade routing and protection. It would be part of his next assignment, he realized only on reaching Washington. Along with the project came a temporary bump to Captain, unheard of in the peacetime Navy. It was the first inkling Eric had of his future roles. The wartime footing the Navy was acquiring and the fact his prior efforts were known or appreciated.

Initially fearful of upsetting her, he was surprised at Christiana's elation at going to Washington. Faced with his first separation from her, he realized how much he loved her. When he initially heard about the assignment, he assumed she would remain in Caracas. That she was happy to join him pleased him. Christiana's only disappointment was that she would need to follow by civilian aircraft rather than join him on the navy plane standing by to bring him to Washington.

Not revealed to her was the supposed danger he was in or the fundamental role Reed played in their lives. Christiana always resented when Reed appeared because it portended another trip by her husband. Before the flurry of activity and transfer, Christiana never questioned his travels nor what he did. Instead, she delighted in teasing him in bed whenever Eric returned, flaunting her breasts and legs in ever more provocative outfits. Inevitably, Eric responded, never quite sure how he lost his usual reticence in the privacy of their bedroom.

Often in a pixie mood, she tried to have sex in other rooms spicing their lovemaking with a hint of danger should servants be about. On most occasions, he managed to wait until they reached their bedroom but once or twice, even Eric could not resist her blandishments, ruining a chair and centuries-old table during their wild gyrations.

From Eric's viewpoint, what Christiana did while he was away troubled him more. Alexandra's nurse was an old family retainer who raised Christiana and looked on her more as a daughter than a mistress. Eric suspected the nurse was perhaps the only person Christiana listened to without raised voice.

Unfortunately, the nurse indulged the girl-child-woman, hiding some of her transgressions from Eric, her father, and Alexandra.

The transfer to Washington pleased Eric. Being away from his country for three years and anxious that Alexandra be exposed to his heritage, he welcomed the change. With an inward smile, he did feel sorry for Washington and the havoc Christiana would wreck on capitol society. He was glad only his mother was not alive to be scandalized. Eric knew now Christiana was everything he was not. But in recognizing this conundrum, he also admitted a central fact about their relationship.

Put simply, he loved her and would tolerate almost anything in her behavior. In the end, Christianna was his wife, the mother of his child, and above all, a unique, glorious, warm-hearted person. Someone who also made him deliriously happy when they were together.

Moving isn't 100% smooth. Eric's and Christina's first fight occurred when she told him Alexandra would not join them until the baby was older. He had accepted she would be their only child, but the joy she gave him almost made up for the recognition he would be the last Eric to go to the Academy. It never crossed his mind that she could go.

In acceding to Christiana's wishes, Eric demanded an English-speaking nanny join the wet nurse in Alexandra's entourage. With the backing of his father-in-law, he won the day.

Over his time in Caracas, he had grown quite fond of El Manipulador, who reciprocated the affection. A shared love for Alexandra, liking for solving puzzles, and intense feelings for Christiana made them co-conspirators in many things involving their families. It was an alliance that lasted until the older man's death.

# December, 1940
## Jonathan Stafonic

On his last day in Caracas, Eric said goodbye to his father-in-law early in the day, cleaned his desk at the embassy, and went home. As he packed his one travel bag, their maid admitted the Ambassador.

The older man came in holding a bottle of scotch. Eric waved him to a seat in the main sitting room, bringing two classes from the liquor cabinet. Alec knew the embassy gossip that Jonathan Stafonic's Foreign Service career was ending.

Four months beyond the end of his rotation cycle, Stafonic's replacement was delayed in Washington due to the impending birth of his first child. As it was, Stafonic's tenure was already long by standard State Department policy. He became Ambassador in 1933. The whisper in diplomatic circles hinted at some transgression never openly discussed.

Alex was also aware that retirement would soon follow upon his return to Washington. Eric recognized how much the Ambassador had done for him personally and professionally with their parting near.

Now the diplomat was facing retirement with little to do but review old dispatches and keepsakes from a 30-odd year career that cost him his wife, two sons, and higher recognition if scuttlebutt was correct. Eric also became aware a similar fate might be awaiting him in their parting.

He had forsworn sea duty to be with Christiana, and promotion would be harder without the right combination of assignments. Was she worth the sacrifice? He thought so but not for the first time recognized the cost.

"Thought we would drink to your leaving," the older man said.

"Celebrate or mourn," Eric replied.

"I should think you'd be glad to get back to the states?"

"My family is here. I don't like leaving them."

43

"It's for your protection."

"I can take care of myself."

"Reed thought he could as well," Stafonic said softly.

"I thought he could too," Eric said soberly, taking a small sip.

"That's why I put my best Marine on your front door tonight. Just in case."

"In case of what?"

"Some people might think your too dangerous to live."

"I'm just a naval officer."

"Whose almost singlehandedly ease merchant shipping to England."

"Says the British Ambassador just last week."

"Good to hear but we suffered a great loss."

"True but he won't be the last before all this is over."

"Do you think we will get involve?"

"We already are in a lot of ways. Our leader is chummy with our Limey friends and they need our help."

"Maybe I can get a seagoing assignment."

"I doubt it for the foreseeable future. They want you in Washington to do for us what you did for the British."

"You think so?"

"If I read the cables right, yes."

While every navy officer covets being Captain, other roles and tasks needed leadership. Over the previous months, he appreciated how his abilities could play out in the coming world crisis. It didn't beget public imagination or glory but contributed to the allied victory.

Stung by what he heard, Eric changed the conversation.

"What will you do when you're relieved," Eric asked.

"Go back to Washington, write by brief on what's happening here and wait for them to show me to the door," Stafonic answered after pondering his response.

"Surely, they could use your expertise?"

"There are people at State who didn't appreciate some intelligence reviews I wrote early this decade."

"About what?"

"I was stationed in Germany as Embassy Secretary but my real assignment was looking East at Russia, Poland, Czechoslovak, the

Balkans. What I saw worried me. I wrote some papers warning about what would happen once Russia turned west."

"And?"

"Well, the pages weren't very flattering to Joseph Stalin. You know, there are some people in State who think he is the savior of the world."

"I hadn't thought much about it."

"Well, now, with this pact he made with Hitler, everyone wonders what he will do."

"But what did you do that upset people."

"Told them not to trust him."

"What happened?"

"Got me posted here without a promotion. That's a sign your career is dead ended."

"But you're an ambassador?"

"That's where luck and the right wife helps."

"Whoa!"

"What has a wife have to do with it?"

"I better go back to the beginning."

"Yes, I know little about you and the embassy staff is very tight lipped."

Taking another long sip from his class, the Stafonic began talking to an enraptured host.

"My father was unhappy in Czechoslovak and wanted to join his brother in the states. Since he was the brightest of the family, many relatives pooled their monies and sent him to America. This was in 1864, and somehow, he got to Indiana in time to join the last enlistments for the Civil War.

With his bounty money, he paid for his brother and two other men to join him. Over time, there was a slew of people from our town smack in the middle of Indiana. When DuPont built a paint manufacturing plant nearby, they all went to work there. Somewhere during that time, my father met my mother. Who her folks were, she never said but seemed happy in my father's heritage?

My older brother liked science and followed him into DuPont from high school. I was luckier. At 18, I was taller and heavier than other boys and enjoyed roughing it. When they formed the town's football team, I became the center, then fullback. The DuPont plant manager was a Princeton grad, and he saw some potential.

Somehow or other, he arranged for me to enroll in Princeton that September. He falsified my high school credentials and convinced my parents tutors at the college would help me get through my studies.

The Spanish-American War had started, and I wanted to go off to fight. My mother stopped me. Said she would disown me if I passed up this chance. So, while my brother went off to Florida, where he promptly died of yellow fever, I went to Princeton.

The narrative was interrupted by Christiana's appearance. Seeing the man comfortably seated, she rushed into the room, embracing him warmly.

"My senor hombre," she giggled happily, using the name she had given him as a young teenager.

"Christiana, it always nice to see you," he replied warmly.

"Always the gentleman. He no like this wild teenager who steal cookies from his embassy," she said using a mocking, heavily accented patois.

"Which you gave to the kids hanging outside our gates," he said, laughing.

"They were too thin."

"I see you haven't lost your figure."

"I did look like a cow."

"Now you are once more enchanting."

"Are you trying to seduce me?" she replied mockingly.

"Like every other man in Caracas."

"I am no longer available, I have my man."

"Indeed you do."

"But now your government is taking him away from me."

"Only temporarily, I assure you."

"One night is too much. But now I leave you two men to your talk. What you talk about bores me. Do not be late, Eric leaves early tomorrow." She said, trailing a whiff of perfume as she left the room with a meaningful glance back at Eric.

After she departed, silence hung in the room for moments as the two men gathered their thoughts.

"You know Eric, all the society mothers of sons in Caracas breathe a sigh of relief when you chose that woman," Stafonic said reflectively.

"She chose me," Eric replied with a laugh.

"Those women all knew she would do the choosing and all knew none of their sons could live up to her demands."

"Her demands are simple."

"Are they?"

"Well, the sun, the moon, the stars."

"Yes, her husband needed to be strong with her but in return?"

"Yes, I know what you mean. It's been one of a hell-of-a-ride."

"Are you sorry?"

"Hell, no!"

"Good answer. Will you have more children?"

"Not possible anymore. Doctors said it would be too dangerous for her."

"Does she know?"

"Yes, she thinks she has disappointed me."

"Has she?"

"No, Alexandra will be enough. Losing her would be too tough. I think we're both one love-in-a-lifetime people."

"Then I wish you much future happiness."

"With this war coming, we're going to need it."

"Yes, Christiana left too soon, I bring greetings and blessings from the archbishop."

"For both of us?"

"Yes, between you and me he gets a big kick out of Christiana. He saw her stealing his wine dressed in the nun's habit. He didn't stop her because he knew there would be a big donation in the poor box. She always paid for her pranks and he knew it."

"Finish your story."

"I will, I think someone is waiting for me to leave."

"I'll sleep on the plane."

"To finish my story, I first saw my wife while looking at the ceiling surrounding her face at some party after my sophomore year's Harvard game. She saw me drunk and dirty with vomit. There were wild parties then, and I was the wildest. The rube from Indiana, thrown in with the society types. So naturally, I had to be more hectic than them. And I was too, till I met her. She changed me. Went from a student who settled for average to some studious gent who happened to play football. By the time I graduated, I was in the top ten percent of my class. We dated for a year before I realized she came from a family with four generations of diplomats. They could do that using the inheritance of three generations of merchant bankers. Her family didn't like her choice of a husband but acceded to her demands that I join the foreign service. We had a great career together until I wrote the one report no one liked. When the Ambassador before me died, she used all of her contacts to make me the logical choice. Then she went and died on me two years ago."

"I am sorry," Eric murmured.

"No need, we had a good life together. But remember, no matter how much we know about our wives, they will always surprise you."

"My does every day."

"And she will continue to every day. Mine taught me a good lesson just before she died. She wanted to buried in my family's plot in Indiana not with her ancestors in Boston. Surprised the hell out of me. So that's where I'm headed when I retire."

"Indiana's as good a place as any," Eric said, not knowing what to reply.

"Yes, but sure put her family's nose out-of-joint."

"Death is a subject we don't talk about especially after Reed's killing."

"He was a casualty of war and he won't be the last," Stafonic said quietly.

"Who do you think ordered it?"

"Your friend Bernadotte."

"He's not my friend and I didn't think he was that important."

"Don't be naïve. He heads German spy operations in several countries if Reed was correct in his analysis."

"I hadn't realized that."

"You didn't need to know."

"But he doesn't act that sinister."

"The mark of a good spy."

"Will anything be done to avenge Reed."

"No, we accept our losses and hope we can turn them to our advantage."

"I have a lot to learn."

"About spy craft yes, about getting supplies where they need to be, no."

"That's just solving problems."

"Which you are good at. But when you go north, you're going to step on some toes."

"I don't think so."

"Yes, Eric, you have a way of thinking that gets results without worrying about what came before. Many people who have jobs think in terms of how things are being done now. When the war comes, and you and I know it will, to win will mean throwing out the book and starting fresh. A lot of people don't know how to forget the book. Here you did it and up there you will need to do it even harder and faster. Your career may suffer but I think you will ultimately have the recognition you earn."

"I hope you're wrong about the opposition."

"We'll see but, in the meantime, remember to do your job the way you see fit regardless of the consequences."

"I'll try."

"You'll succeed and with that I will leave you to the lady waiting down the hall. I'll see myself out."

The older man got up from his chair and passed the marine sentry. He nodded to the Marine, who went to attention. The Ambassador gave him a half-salute and went to his car half-drunk but pleased he had given his thoughts to Eric. The rest was up to him.

# December, 1940
## Christiana Dykman

All Caracas marveled at the whirlwind life Christiana Dykman continued to live even after her marriage. Following the usual pattern, most speculation was of the negative 'Tsk Tsk' sort. Ignoring for the moment questions about her loyalty to the marriage bed, many older mothers wondered if the still young beauty was paying enough attention to her daughter, Alexandra.

Archly, more dowagers questioned what her husband thought about the late-night carousing and daily encounters with the young wealthy crowd she knew almost from the cradle or who had recently appeared as the country prospered. What the observers ignored was her practically total abstinence from liquor.

These younger businessmen saw that the belligerents' demands would require ever more significant resources at inflated prices. They often pumped Christiana for clues, but she ignored them, preferring to remain coy about what Eric said or did. For, in truth, he told her little.

Venezuela's oil was perhaps the biggest prize for both sides, ore, and meats close behind. These commodities required strategies for getting them to the war zones. Shipping rates soared along with the demands. Caraccas' social elites, Christiana's brothers included, stood ready to supply and ship them at inflated prices.

The changing maritime situation did not escape either Eric or Reed. Both feared the German efforts to clear as many cargoes as possible from South American ports before any hostilities needed to be chronicled and slowed. No one was better at ferreting out German efforts than Reed, and Eric's role was to stymie them as much as possible. Together they made a formidable team.

A side effect of their efforts was the tight circle of cooperation that drew them closer than either had ever imagined. To some extent, Christiana suffered some neglect. Extremely busy on the tasks Reed assigned him almost daily, Eric sometimes was away for a week or more.

Happily, the neglect did not diminish her ardor for the American. Whether gone a day or a week, his return always elicited yelps of joy from his still new wife. Denying him food, she ushered them into their bedroom at whatever hour he returned, not letting him go for hours.

Always surprised at his own responses to her advances, Eric never needed to initiate any lovemaking. Coupled with her spontaneity, these encounters elicited moments of sheer delight. These spasms of joy were unknown to him before their meeting. In their lovemaking and togetherness, Despite his frequent absences, Christiana time and again demonstrated her total commitment to the man she married when he returned.

Besotted as they both were, neither had doubts of their mutual attraction. With a certainty that belied her age, at the moment they met, Christiana realized she would need to be the aggressor. From the moment she saw him, they were bound together. They never spoke of her aggressive nature at the embassy. Both knew it was necessary, he would never have approached her.

That dynamic continued to play in their love making. If he held back, she would tease him, wiggle her hips provocatively and become even more amorous. This never failed to arouse him. He knew never would he have ever approached her.

Like other aspects of their marriage, neither acknowledged the truth. But both knew that she had chosen him. Given this fact, Christiana also knew she could never leave this marriage. It was the first time she did not chafe at some chain holding her back in her life.

Given his work, there were few times the couple could or wanted to be seen in public. This suited Eric, but the Ambassador interceded to suggest an occasional night out. With an excellent grasp of the city's social antenna, he knew what others thought of the marriage, which could be changed through a few public appearances. A wise judge of people, he knew anyone who saw them together would recognize the besotted looks they gave each other.

Caracas society wondered at the marriage but not her Duane. She was satisfied all was well when stripping the bed after their lovemaking before the household entered the room or picking up their strewn clothes.

The Duane was also aware of Christiana's fervent desire not to have more children. The older woman was cognizant that Eric did not comprehend the depth of his wife's fears. It was enough for her to know. Christiana's commitment to be a willing participant in this wild love affair and not desire another man or baby.

Christiana and Eric knew the strength of their bond within months of the wedding. A glue holding them together until death.

Their daughter was the only intruder world capable of coming between them. Like her mother, Alexandra recognized her father even at this young age. An unbreakable link between father and daughter was forged by her first birthday. A link tested in life but never broken.

Of her mother, Alexandra's ties were less binding. The duenna who had reared Christiana was now charged with her second generation. It was a role the Duane willingly accepted to stay close to the mother she had seen grow from the cradle.

Indeed, the Duanne was the only person besides Eric who could remonstrate Christiana to the point of the younger woman listening. Did the woman heed all the advice or orders either suggested? Not by a long shot. But enough to keep the Duane happy.

Christiana was by nature a flirt and continued in that mode even after marriage. But like a Geisha, she promised much more than was delivered. When Eric was away, Christiana would indulge in a night of carousing with the playmates of her teen years.

Fueled by drinks which she totally declined, these lotharios would playfully woo her. Encouraged by her bantering replies, some even accompanied her home. All went away frustrated, left at the door of her home bought for the couple by her father.

Keeping score were her envious girlfriends, many of whom got a vicarious thrill out of the small measure of revenge inflicted on the men of the male-dominated culture. As the war heated u, fortunes were being made in oil, manufacturing, livestock, and shipping by a group of Venezuelan men dedicated to using their newfound wealth to sample the supposedly sheltered upper-class woman.

These social climbers saw in Christiana the ultimate sexual prize. Naturally welcoming, she engaged them in the same manner as was her wont with older friends. Many mistook the banter for flirtation and thought they were clues to more serious romance. Christiana always had the ultimate fallback play when someone became more insistent: "My husband expects me home."

If a would-be suitor got too aggressive, as happened a time or two, a well-placed knee cooled their ardor.

When Eric announced the move to the United States, Christiana was pleased at first. Then realizing the separation from friends, family, and Alexandra, her exuberance turned to fear.

"What if they don't like me? She cried to Eric in their bed.

"Who are they?"

"The people we will meet. Your friends. Fellow officers. The admirals who decide your career."

"You decided my career at the embassy party. I'm a shore side sailor from here on in."

"Oh Erik are you so sure?"

"I've missed two seagoing tours, now have a specialty in short supply with even shorter promotion opportunities."

"Erik, I am so sorry."

"I'm not. I have you, Alexandra and a very interesting assignment."

"What is this assignment."

"Christiana, I can't tell you but trust me I am happier than I ever thought possible."

"Are you sure?"

"Surer than anything else in this world."

She jumped on him again, and they said no more between their moans.

After Eric left, Christiana planned to follow in a few days flying by Pan Am Clipper. Herself fluent in four languages, she wanted her daughter to be multi-lingual. Christiana also wanted Alexandra to learn the language spoken in England.

An English accent indicated high breeding regardless of the speaker's background in the Caracas of the 1930s. Often, Christiana threw in American idioms learned from her teachers and nuns at the various schools she attended. Having been rejected by the best secondary schools because of her hijinks, Christiana wanted her daughter to be more sedate. As she told the Duane, "God forbid she should be like me. The poor thing."

For help, she turned to the woman most remote from her life, her mother. Antigone Longbottom De la Vega was born in England to a minor English noble family long on history but short of monies. Raised in genteel poverty that only the British know how to carry off, she loved her home county Dales with their windswept hills, harsh winters, sweet springs, and glorious summers.

Resigned to marrying a local gentry, her life changed when she met Christiana's father. Dashing, urbane, intelligent, he was touring the Dales seeking breeding stock for a cattle ranch planned for the Southern Venezuelan backcountry. Antigone joined her father in Enrique's tour of their farm, stables, and house. His eye did not miss the signs of neglect and lack of funds. Nor did they overlook the figure in jodhpurs who supplemented her father's commentary.

Then as always in his life, Enrique was a man willing to see beyond the obvious. Enrique fell immediately in love with Antigone. Raised by a doting father whose only son preferred men to women in his bed, she was not beautiful or delicate but strong-featured, wholesome-looking, light-skinned, and forthright in speech and action. Antigone could ride, shod, groom a horse, and then ride him herding cattle, sheep, or pigs. She was able to shoot like a man and drink most under the table but came to their marriage bed unsure of any womanly skills.

Older by 10 years and raised in the hothouse sexual world of the Caracas elite and sure of her view of country manners and animal husbandry, Enrique assumed Antigone knew more of human bed encounters than was the case. Their courtship was a whirlwind, and the wedding was swiftly arranged in the Dales church, where she was baptized. Leaving her heartbroken father, they boarded ship for South America two days later, the marriage still unconsummated.

In a reversal of the usual dowry negotiation, Enrique settled on his father-in-law a pension enabling him to remain in his ancestral home for the rest of his life. When he died after the war, Enrique wanted to keep the estate, but British death duties forced the sale of the manor. Enrique's continued support of Antigone's brother enabled him to live in genteel poverty before ending his life in a London bedsitter just before the turn of the 20th century.

While the best suite on the boat, their cabin was hardly the place for such a momentous event. They put off everything remotely connected to sex until in the bridal suite of the best hotel, the Luxor, in Caracas. Having seen many a barn coupling, Antigone was unprepared for Enrique's strength or desire. For him, it was two days of delight, for her horror. Nor did their lovemaking become easier over time and through her first two births. Their sons delighted Enrique while she dreaded more children.

Antigone sought refuge in what she knew, running a large estate. By dint of her work and leadership, their ranch became a model for the country. The couple divided the households over the years, seemingly and naturally separated by their duties. She remained down in the country, coming to the capital less and less. Enrique spent more and more time with his other investments and companies. When the boys needed to go to high school, they moved in with their father.

Content with his two boys, Enrique did not seek Antigone's marital bed until the spring of 1917, when he and the boys were there to celebrate the annexation of acreage, almost doubling the ranch's size. At the end of the evening, Enrique followed Antigone into her bed chamber and forcefully took her in such a way that she responded for the first time. There followed a night of lovemaking that pleased them both. A month later, to Antigone's surprise, she was pregnant with Christiana. Outwardly angry but secretly pleased, she told Enrique while banishing him forever from her bed.

A shocked Enrique accepted both pieces of news, not knowing how to deal with either. That he still loved Antigone was obvious to him. Would he try to change her mind? His Latin pride would not allow him to beg or implore. But for reasons he did not understand, he insisted on taking a young girl from the ranch as Duane and wet nurse for Christiana. He never returned to the country property turning it over to Antigone and giving her an unlimited bank account.

Through the years, Antigone appeared only for special occasions or when Christiana's hijinks resulted in some crisis. Enrique and his wife forged a relationship that served them well at critical junctures in Christiana's life. Indulged by her father, Christiana always resented the distance her mother kept while she reached maturity. Mother and daughter suspected Christiana's wild behavior was partly due to the need for her mother's attention. Regardless, Antigone stayed at the ranch, which she loved almost as much as her children. With the birth of her grandchild, she began to rethink and regret her decisions.

When she chose Eric, Christiana did not talk with her mother but asked her to intercede for permission to marry. Eric's encounters with Antigone were few but cordial. Seeing her daughter's happiness and refraining from drinking, she eventually approved of the match.

It was at her ranch the couple stayed after the wedding. Antigone knew there would be no more children, seeing her daughter's difficult pregnancy and childbirth. Already a grandmother of three through her sons, she was pleased her daughter would add to the family.

The baby quickly became Antigone's favorite grandchild. She dreaded the day her granddaughter left the country. Happily, she was able to find a way for her to remain at the ranch until that day.

English expatriates often banded together for mutual support and succor when in foreign lands throughout the world. Venezuela was no different, and Christiana sensed her mother might know someone to join her household. Her query brought an immediate response but with-it tragedy.

# February, 1940

## Gertrude Seaman

Tea shops looking strangely out of place in cities worldwide catered to English expatriates and travelers seeking familiar surroundings in distant lands. With chintz curtains, delicate teacups, scone-based offerings, "cuppa o tea," these shops attracted repeat trade by being more English than their domestic counterparts. Outdated newspapers lined walls, and issues already debated and settled in Parliament were still argued in gentile surroundings.

In Caracas, there was one such establishment, *Ye Olde Tea Garden*. By 1940 it was run by Gertrude Seaman on Calle O'Higgins. Since it first opened in 1911, the meeting place was owned by a succession of displaced English women who found themselves deposited on Venezuelan shores. Either voluntarily or for other reasons, they chose to remain in South America for one reason or another. Usually, the proprietress ended their tenure through marriage, frequently to another displaced emigre from the Isles.

When the last owner in 1937 was selling up, British intelligence swooped in and bought the shop assigning one of their most reliable agents to run it. Called Gertie, Gertrude Seaman celebrated what she considered her 40th birthday at the beginning of 1939. It was also her 20th year with the intelligence establishment, which recruited, trained, and used her in many countries.

Unsure of her antecedents, Gertie's only parental memory was her mother trading her to the London whorehouse when she was 11 in return for fare back to Birmingham. Waifish in appearance, for nine years, Gertie was featured dressed in little girl costumes in sex dramas for which the porn house enjoyed an underground reputation. Claiming she owed the whorehouse money for her mother and her board, Gertie, like many other women in her situation, was always in debt to the establishment. An obligation reinforced by terror from two pimps, always on guard against girls leaving.

In her teens, the men and conditions hardened her into an emotionless doll who disassociated herself from the sexual events she experienced. Souring of the life and people around her, she rebelled against its pimps in an explosion of violence. One night, she slashed one pimp, and used a broken bottle to kill a patron. Along the way, she avoided motherhood through two abortions. Clearly psychotic by age 20, Gertie was rapidly becoming a liability to her Soho whorehouse. Shrewdly, one regular patron thought Gertie might be better used in the secret service, where her elastic morals might be better employed. One night, as she grudgingly serviced him, he gave her an address and an appointment time.

Stealing away one morning but unsure of his reasons for helping her, she ventured to the address on the card. Whisked away to a country estate outside London, Gertie satisfied a battery of tests and probing interviews. The government department bought her contract from the establishment, and she went for training at their facility in Scotland. Proving amazingly flexible in the use of force and her womanly skills, in the post-World War I spy world, she gained a reputation for ruthlessness and cunning,

Unfortunately, by 1935, Gertie was becoming more a liability than an asset as she had no restraint in using sometimes lethal force to gain the group's goals. This propensity culminated in Rome when she killed two Papal Guards while trying to photograph correspondence between the Holy See and Berlin. Escaping undetected, her quick resort to violence worried senior bureaucrats, still tightrope walking with German authorities. Sending her to Caracas seemed an excellent solution for what was at that time perceived as a backwater part of the world.

Before leaving London, Gertie paid calls on the two now-retired pimps from the whore house, leaving both dead and police with no clues as to their murderer.

Arriving in Caracas, Gertie first played the young widow and quickly became the romantic objective of some key Venezuelan officials. Playing them off of each other, she was soon ensconced in the everyday social life of the rapidly expanding city. Using British government funds, she bought the tea shop and quickly turned it into an international meeting place where English exiles and Venezuelan elites met and discussed news from England and the world. From this

58

flow, Gertie was able to start building an information tree not only about Venezuela but other South American countries.

Belatedly, officials in London began to see the importance South America would play in the coming conflict they now realized was inevitable. She was ordered to expand her spy network, Gertie started recruiting agents to blanket the continent. By the beginning of 1939, much to the chagrin of the London establishment, she was de facto head of British spy operations on the continent. She was loath to give up this position even when twice replacement agents were sent.

Both times they reported back her refusal to turn over the network. Hoping to avoid creating more disunion, they confirmed Gertie in the role.

As a woman, Gertie created a circle of expatriate single and married women who congregated at her shop where they could gossip and gain strength from each other. It was to this group that young women like Deborah de Courcy came. Keeping a wary eye on romances across economic and geographic separation, she was able to head off several potentially harmful endings for British and American embassy workers. By the same token, she encouraged several liaisons which benefited her country's espionage efforts.

Unfortunately, her tendency to act violently when more subtle means were available infuriated her masters at the Embassy and London. Only when her expeditious handling of Deborah's affair proved immensely valuable did her bosses begin the see her value. In the end, her Caracas posting led to a lifelong career in his Majesty's service.

Without her identifying events beforehand and turning them to Britain's advantage, the Italians and Germans could have staged a significant spy coup.

Alerted to a recent breach at the British embassy, they told her to find some way of discrediting the information in Italian and German eyes. The security people at the enemy were also concerned about the woman who had, in their opinion, inadvertently provided the information needed to breach its defenses.

Her fate was also given to Gertie to sort out. She suspected they expected her to eliminate the woman. Gertie was looking for other solutions for the poor lady who had the misfortune of falling in love with the wrong person.

# November, 1940
## Deborah de Courcy

Deborah de Courcy never thought she would be in a foreign land, without a pound or peso, and in fear. Yet all three things were happening to her, and she had nowhere to turn.

Raised just outside London, she attended Oxford on scholarship earning an A level in economics. In this decade and these times, this was no mean achievement for a woman. But the cost had been high. Her family disapproved, expecting her to marry and raise children. In particular, her mother's jealousy drove her to a low-paid ministry position rather than the academic career she dreamed of as a teenager.

When offered a posting to Venezuela, she grabbed at it, hoping to improve her prospects through the experience.

Arriving in the capital before Christmas 1939 and lonely with few friends, Deborah met Vittorio Massaro three months into her Caracas stay. Vaguely connected to the Italian embassy, he ardently wooed her with promises of romances. Emotionally scarred by her academic affairs, she initially spurned his advances. Eventually succumbing to his charms, Deborah began spending more and more time with the handsome native of Rome. He artfully plied her with questions about the embassy and its staff, always vague about his duties.

Returning one Monday from an overnight excursion in the hills, Deborah was greeted by the embassy's security officer. She was taken to a small side office and confronted by senior staff leaders.

"Where have you been?" was the first question thrown at her.

"With whom?"

"If you must know even though it's none of your business Vittorio Massario."

"Do you know who he is?"

"He hangs around at the Italian embassy."

"Doing what?"

"Something to do with not having a visa to return to Italy."

"Is that what he told you."

"In a roundabout way. We don't talk about our jobs or problems."

"Are you sure about that?"

"I know little about his problems. We talk of other things."

"He doesn't ask about our workings?"

"I've had the anti-spy briefings, I don't discuss anything outside the embassy."

"He seems to have known about us."

"What do you mean?"

"While you were away, the embassy was breached and our diplomatic codes photographed."

"Are you sure, and what does that have to do with Vittorio?

"We have our ways of knowing and your friend is really head of Italian espionage here,"

"You're wrong."

"We've been on about him for months. Almost from the start of his romance with you."

"You're wrong about Vittorio."

"You know he has a wife and child in Rome and works with the Italian foreign spy establishment?"

"Of course not. If I had known do you think I would have kept seeing him?"

"That's what we are here to find out."

For 12 hours, Deborah slogged through question after question. Finally satisfied with her answers but not with her actions, they let her depart. She went home to cry on her bed, unsure what was next for her. Startled awake by the knock on the door, Deborah was surprised to hear Vittorio's soft voice calling out.

"Let me in please," he said gently.

"Go away. Don't speak to me."

"But I must. I am leaving and want to say how much I will miss you."

"Miss me? They are sending me home next week. No career. Nothing. A failure."

"For that I am sorry but you must know how I feel about you."

"And your wife? Your child? Your job?"

"They are but nothing to me. You must know that."

61

"I know only you betrayed me and my country. Go away."

"Please let me in so I can show you how much I love you."

Hesitating behind the door, she thought and cried. After a few minutes, she unbolted the door and let Vittorio in.

"M'y amore, I will miss you."

"I don't see why," Deborah said in anguish.

"Because I have come to love you."

"You betrayed me and made them all suspicious of me, of you, or our relationship."

"Surely they do not suspect me."

"Of course they do. I don't know what secrets you got from me but it is enough to make them send me home in disgrace."

"I am just a poor man adrift in a foreign country."

"They don't believe that nor do I."

"Are you sure."

"Do you see these red eyes? These soiled clothes for the last 12 hours I have been answering their questions."

"But you are here?"

"Only until the next boat to England."

"I see," the Italian said, looking away from her, processing what she had said.

Coming to a decision based on this latest statement, he turned back around, grabbing her by the neck to strangle the threat to his mission. Surprised, she fought him, moving back into the small area that served as her kitchen.

A knife lay on the table. Desperately, Deborah grabbed it and, without thinking, plunged it into his stomach. He continued to move forward, hands reaching for her throat. Still frightened, she swung the knife again, this time at his face. Shock, perplexity, and anger crossed his facial features. Blindly and without thought guiding her hand, the blade cut through his throat, spouting arterial blood onto her face and dress.

Vittorio slumped to the floor, his life's blood draining out in seconds. Deborah looked at the body, throwing away the knife, and wept.

Within minutes of gathering her thoughts, Deborah changed clothes leaving the blood-smeared garments on the floor. Packing her small briefcase, she walked around the body and exited the apartment.

Scared, angry at his betrayal, and unsure of the embassy's reaction, Deborah called the only person she felt would help, the English library and tea shop owner. Without realizing it, she had reached the in-country British spymaster. Gertie Seaman.

Having identified Vittorio Massaro as an Italian agent almost from his first day, Gertie shrewdly teased out, Deborah was his target early on. Not knowing who to trust and unsure of others at the embassy, Deborah unknowingly petitioned the only person who could help her.

Gertie had warned the embassy about Deborah and Vittorio but thought the embassy's approach when the theft was discovered too ham-fisted

She would have played the Italian but was overruled.

But the changed circumstances meant there were new opportunities to salvage the situation. To be sure, no one expected Deborah to kill the foreign agent, but Gertie thought they could turn the disaster to Britain's advantage. But the first step was to stash Deborah away from everyone.

Picking up Deborah, she drove directly to Antigone's ranch. Assuring the younger woman of her silence, she left the dazed murderess in the hands of the ranch owner. Their conversation in English sounded like three women having tea. But Antigone and Gertie knew real consequences would happen.

On the ride back, Gertie assessed how to handle what promised to be a complicated international situation. Being an excellent spymaster, along the road, she conceived a plan to turn the murder to the Brits' advantage. Arriving back in Caracas and determining that the body had not been discovered, she asked for help. Two Embassy men came to secretly take Vittorio's body away for private disposal. While this was going on, two other men helped her clean the apartment. When it was sanitized, one was left to discreetly monitor the rooms for the next few days.

Meanwhile, Deborah was reported as missing without official approval from official authorities. Besides the official search, Eleanor put about that she thought the young woman had eloped with Vittorio.

When Vittorio failed to return from some private errand, his clandestine comrades began to worry. Initially, they thought he had gone on another amorous escapade and something he was well known for in the service.

When days passed, and Gertie's story was picked up at the Italian and German embassies, efforts were made to find the couple. Like all spy organizations, the Italians and Germans were not caring about either but worried their recent coup might have been compromised. Their disappearance put into question whether the codes so painstakingly acquired were authentic. Time and efforts were made to verify them, delaying their transmission to Rome and Berlin. After months of analysis, the purloined codes were considered genuine. Given the delay, the English had changed the code. The Axis powers could read past cables but not future transmissions.

Deborah remained at the ranch, unaware of her government's efforts to turn the tragedy into an intelligence coup. Nervous at what she had done. Unsure of how the Embassy people were reacting and scared as to her future. When weeks turned into months, the fears grew.

Finally, Gertie came to visit. She assured Deborah no crime was being ascribed to her but returning to the Foreign Service was impossible. Through Gertie, a tiny stipend would be given to Deborah until another opportunity was found. Along with the assistance was the need for the younger woman to be discreet for the following year. After that time, she was free to do anything, but normal positions involving her economic studies were not possible.

During their time together, Antigone came to like her guest, and when Christiana asked for help in finding an English tutor, Deborah was the natural choice. Of course, that meant Alexandra needed to stay at the ranch, which inordinately pleased her grandmother.

Assured she had carried out her husband's wishes, Christiana happily left for Washington. Whether the capital was ready for her or not, she was prepared for it.

# December, 1940
## Sven Bernadotte

Knowing there was money to be had when he appeared, stevedores across South America welcomed the Swedish gentlemen who acted so German. With him came bags of money distributed liberally when his needs were met. His requests were always seemingly modest: an unregistered item to the loading process, changing the destination information on a ship's manifest, allowing an unrecorded visit onboard a guarded vessel. There was always someone ready to help the Nordic visitor, whatever the need.

Twice British agents almost caught Sven during his clandestine placing of incendiary devices on merchant ships before they sailed. One device apparently worked as the vessel was lost to fire three days from port. He did not know if his other attempts at sabotage were successful. To his amusement, the British placed a thousand-pound reward for his identity.

Aside from being described as tall, blond-haired, and stout, they had little to go on. Reed kept insisting their enemy was Sven Bernadotte, but his English counterparts weren't so sure.

Concurrently, Sven's German handlers were happy with the number of vessels arriving in Sweden and Spain with vital war supplies. They were so pleased he was given a crucial extra duty. Identifying ways Venezuelan oil could be obtained again through Sweden or Spain. With it came a request by the German high command for more information on American defenses of the Panama Canal and north-south trade routes.

Sven set up an oil import-export firm with offices in Caracas, Lima, Rio, and Montevideo to do the former. Locals were hired as secretaries in each location while the managing directors were part of his spy ring. Their assignment was to purchase oil and find ways of diverting cargoes to neutral countries.

At a Caracas business party, he learned of an American courier returning with contingency plans involving three South American navies to coordinate with the US Navy. Identifying the officer from the US Embassy in Brazil, Sven and his team intercepted him on his way to the Rio airport, killing the guard, driver, and courier. After cutting the sealed pouch from the man's dead wrist, Sven and his men fled. When examined, the pouch's contents were considered so important they were on the way to Germany on the next Luft Hansa plane. The murder was never solved, but Sven received kudos from Berlin.

Sven developed a reputation for carrying out challenging, i.e., bloody, assignments better than most of his contemporaries within spy ranks. His abilities were not lost by his German spymasters.

As he flitted about the continent, one British agent started a file about him. Gertie Seaman's success in the Vittorio Massario affair gave her the capital to branch out. Soon she was running agents in four South American countries and providing London with much helpful information.

# December, 1940
## Eric Dykman

Tired, unshaved, and in a rumpled uniform from the three-day flight from Caracas, Eric was surprised the Navy staff car brought him to the Ordinance building serving as Navy headquarters. Hoping to sleep and clean up before reporting for duty, it was almost 8pm on a warm night, and he stood in front of a building ablaze with lights and open windows. His frayed military identification wallet showed only his last rank, and the driver was needed to verify his credentials. After consulting a list on his desk, the guard called another sailor to escort him. Barking out the destination, the second sailor seemed startled and looked at Eric dubiously.

"Follow me, sir," he said, half chortling.

"What's funny," Eric demanded.

"You look a little out of uniform and unshaven."

"Been on a plane for three days and brought right here."

"Usually happens that way. Brass has a habit of not wanting to wait for others to spiff up."

"Where we going?"

"You'll see," the sailor cut off the discussion by moving in front and leaving Eric to follow without another word.

Confusing Eric as they snaked through a warren of offices, they arrived at an outer office manned by a guard and Warrant Officer immaculate in dress blues. Looking at the poorly dressed Eric, they indicated he wait standing while the guard knocked softly on the door. The harsh voice told them to send in the new arrival from within.

Opening the door for Eric, the guard nodded him into the office. Inside, Eric saw three Admirals seated around the only desk with an Army general ensconced in a corner.

Washington wardrooms and officers' clubs where naval ranks gathered when discussions turned to preparing to meet Admiral Ernest N. King for the first time disclosed unanimity high in uncertainty. Most such encounters unnerved officers of all ranks, and not a few flag officers had careers sidetracked by his blunt questions.

Sitting behind the small desk devoid of papers except for a manila folder and an officer's career jacket, King looks as formidable as Eric remembered him from the three times they had met previously. At this moment in time, he was head of the Atlantic Fleet but was expected to become Chief of Naval Operations.

"Welcome to Washington, Dykman," King said softly. So softly, it surprised the younger officer.

"Had a long trip?"

"Yes, sir," replied Eric, unsure whether he should stand or sit in the only empty chair in the room. Eric thought the office was extremely small for the head of the Atlantic Fleet.

"We were talking about South America and the Caribbean, convoys and what not and when I heard you were coming in thought it might be a good thing to have you here."

"As you wish. Can I ask who is at this meeting."

"No you can't. They all outrank you. Have jobs to do and you have information they need. Fellow in the corner is from General Marshall's staff. He's here to listen too."

Knowing it was unusual for King to ever let an Army officer on his turf, Eric was impressed by how easily the Army general sat in the office.

First, I'm bumping you two ranks to Commander," King said. "Should have happened sooner, from what I hear. "

"Not enough sea duty."

"Sometimes it's not needed. Hear you got along well with the Limeys?

"If you mean the Brits yes."

"How'd you, do it? Can't stand them myself."

"Some of them can get your back, Sir. But always phrase everything in ways that benefit them. Do that, and it's impressive the cooperation.

"I'll keep that in mind. Now what about convoys. You sent ships out alone."

"Yes sir. The Germans couldn't send many subs to South America and it's a long passage. Where you need convoys is closer to the continent. There aren't enough convoy protection vessels available to the Brits. So, they need to bunch the ships up into a convoy when they get closer to land."

"Still going to lose ships."

"Part of getting them through is speed. A convoy can only go as fast as its slowest ship. Convoys need at least 11 knots to have a chance. Some of the ships the Brits chartered could turn 10 knots with a following wind."

"What about loading cargo."

"You need to have a plan for each ship that takes into account what's needed most and eases unloading as each item is unloaded. Labor peace on the dock is also important. And more importantly unless I miss my guess, we don't have enough supply ships to sustain an Army Corps let alone two or more which are going to be needed in Europe."

For the first time, the Army general spoke, "George said the same thing to the President and Secretary Knox.

"What's your solution?" King barked at Eric.

"Don't have one yet but I'll go find some answers."

"You just outlined your job but don't expect any help from the Supply people. They still think any war will be over when our battleships appear."

"I don't think so, Sir." Eric said.

"Neither do I Commander," addressing Eric with his new title.

For the next hour, from memory, Eric outlined and gave details about the efforts he and others undertook in South America. Several times, the Admirals asked technical questions about routing, convoy assignments, British successes, and failures in shepherding ships across the Atlantic.

Eric only faltered talking about Reed, and the other casualties in the quiet war waged the past two years. As the meeting closed, he finally remembered to thank Admiral King for his promotion.

Brushing the thank you aside, King said the officer had earned the promotion. Adding harshly, Eric would need the rank to deal with issues in his next assignment.

"Go find me answers to those obstacles you've identified, I didn't promote you to sit around on your backside," King finally barked in a way indicating the task would be difficult.

"I'm ready as soon as I can change and find a desk."

"Down the hall and to the right. BOQ is across the yard but I'm thinking that wife of yours will want better accommodations."

King's knowledge of his wife surprised him, which implied he could live in civilian quarters. The Army General added prophetic words.

"Not that you'll get to see much of her," he said grimly.

# March, 1941
## Christiana de la Vega Dykman

Akin to joining a traveling circus was how, later in life, a now-grown teenage friend described accompanying Christiana Dykman, nee de la Vega, anywhere. Remembering their excursions fondly, she spoke of how the spirited, unafraid young woman was constantly adding to her entourage, picking up young and old companions alike.

In more sedate times, this friend described their odysseys as moveable parties on wheels with Christiana as driver and tour director to Caracas peers.

"If we stayed in one place 10 minutes, others gathered. Let the halt last 20 minutes, and it was soon a party. If we spent more time in one place, the party became an all-night affair," the friend often recounted with glee.

No differences in her habit of acquiring new acquaintances appeared while making her way in the air from Caracas via Barranquilla to the United States. The attractive, vivacious woman soon became the center of attraction at every stop, whether airfield or hotel. Nor were usually jaded airline employees immune from her charms. Violating all company rules, the pilots invited her into the forward cabin. She sat in the pilot's seat of the S-40 Boeing called the *Southern Clipper* on the Jamaica-to Miami leg.

These gay conversations and flirtations across the Caribbean filled up the five days of flying. Switching to the rails after arriving in Miami, new companions accompanied her north to Washington. Arriving in the capital two days before Easter in 1941, she followed her father's instructions to contact the Venezuelan ambassador.

When first he got Enrique's request for help looking out for his still young daughter, the Venezuelan Ambassador smothered a huge sigh. Having known Christiana most of her life, the Venezuelan diplomat feared the problems her madcap ways presented to his diplomatic objectives. He knew Christiana was a joy and a devil in one body, and he also fully expected to be answering for some of those transgressions.

Savoring the memories of past escapades committed by Christiana as he held the cable in his hand, he smiled. Then he shuddered, thinking of the consternation in store for Washington society. Shrugging his shoulders, he joyfully went about helping find a home for the offspring of his childhood friend.

Christiana's first need was to find living quarters like all newcomers to the city. Concerned about the upcoming scarcity in rental space facing any newcomer was the rapid growth in Washington as it prepared for war. The Ambassador thought carefully for the decision involved others as well.

Not wanting her too close to the embassy but in the heart of capitol society, choosing her home invited care. Good properties appropriate for an heiress known for outrageous acts, and he feared her reputation would proceed her arrival. Owning her own home meant she could not be evicted for any transgressions he knew Christiana was capable of committing.

The ambassador also knew her wealth and social position would give her entry into old Washington society. That prospect was a two-headed sword, and it would keep Christiana occupied. Her reputation for outrageous acts would also attract some of the more unsavory members of that social class. He only hoped her husband could keep a tighter rein on her than his friend had done while she was growing up. Sighing once again, he recognized the only person who could control Christiana was Christiana.

Hoping she would only be a dull roar, he knew Washington society would not be as forgiving as Caracas elites for anything she did while residing in the new center of the world.

Thanks to a tip, he found an excellent house just off Dupont Circle.

After inspecting it and talking to business people and real estate experts, the Ambassador made a firm bid accepted by the sellers, in this case, an estate executor. Enrique's instructions put no limit on the Ambassador's budget. But even he winced at the price demanded by the estate's attorneys. High for Washington in those pre-war days, it proved a bargain compared to sale prices just two years later.

Four stories with an aerie loft on the roof, the house's first two floors admitted guests through the front door above the cellar kitchen, laundry, and servant quarters. A separate third-floor apartment was reached via inside hallway stairs, while the rear outside stairs and porch allowed private entrance to the fourth-floor living unit. Access to the aerie was only through this last apartment.

Cleverly, the Ambassador listed the house as a two-family arrangement and was added as an official residence of his staff. Divided into four separate living units but listed only as a twin, the Ambassador anticipated wartime requirements related to hogging living quarters.

This far-sighted intervention on his part saved Eric and Christiana much grief during the war. At one time, her father, the Duenas, Deborah DeCourcy, and assorted brothers, their wives, children, and others camped out in the four-story building. It remained Eric's home address until his retirement. Alexandra also considered the house her childhood home even though she attended and stayed at the famed Madeira boarding school.

Tired but eager to see Eric, Christiana arrived at the Washington railroad station only to be disappointed. In place of Eric was the Venezuelan Ambassador apologizing for the officer's absence at meetings in Norfolk. They proceeded in his official car to her new home. Christiana immediately loved the house, pleasing the older man. Despite her fatigue and displaying her usual ebullience, she hugged him, pronouncing the house a dream come true.

She ran through the house exclaiming its virtues until she reached the aerie. Commandeering it immediately for her husband and herself, it remained her refuge for the rest of her life. The Ambassador assured Christiana Eric would return by nightfall. She shooed him out to take a bath. Surprised she was hungry after the bath, the well-stocked refrigerator, including champaign, and pantry attested to the thoroughness of the diplomat's sagacity.

When Eric arrived that night, Christiana wasted no time leading him to their enclave, where they made love until the dawn hour, at which point he needed to slip away. His rumpled suit was the butt of many comments that next day until he could retrieve new clothes for the BOQ where he was staying. Impatiently, he returned to the house

73

they both would come to love. No one else, not even their daughter, ever slept in their alcove.

The diplomatic counselor's help enabled Christiana to go about hiring staff and commissioning a chef, maid, and chauffeur. The last was needed because she was on the suspended driver list in Caracas, and neither the Ambassador nor her husband trusted her to safely navigate the city's streets. But the chauffeur required a car to drive, and one was secured.

At Christiana's insistence, a bright Yellow Buick specially painted for her became the family car. Not wanting to withstand the jibes of his fellow officers, Eric usually took a cab to work. Before having the car painted, he tried to change her mind. But like himself, Christiana could be stubborn. As to the reason for the color selection, she told Eric the bright yellow would enable her to see it better. To himself, he thought she wanted to make sure everybody saw her.

Like her family, friends, trade people, and ordinary citizens, Eric agreed with her whims because they basically did not hurt anyone and pleased her. Pleasing her was one of the great pleasures in his life. In addition, Eric could never withstand her low laugh, and she won many arguments by simply laughing about them. Once that happened, the disagreement seemed so small as not worth fighting over.

# January, 1941
## Deborah de Courcy

In the months following Vittorio Massaro's death, Antigone de la Vega was manna from heaven for Deborah de Courcy. Soothing the economist's fears and adding her to the household staff did away with any immediate heartaches. She did not hear from the embassy except for one curt call telling her to remain at the ranch.

Located seven hours from Caracas, the ranch lay on Venezuelan pampas still sparsely settled because of the periodic malaria epidemics which killed thousands. An hour's drive separated her property from the nearest settlement. When his wife chose to settle here, Enrique arranged for the extension of telephone lines to the house and installed multiple auxiliary power setups. Many other improvements were constructed in and around the multi-thousand acres as new land was added to the original purchase. Antigone added rooms to her home and built separate compounds for her sons. Her advent led to improved education, infrastructure, and employment opportunities for surrounding villages.

Doting on her daughter's child, Antigone installed the baby in rooms next to her bed-chamber. Much to her sons' annoyance, and despite having other grandchildren, Alexandra was clearly her favorite. Why this was the case, Antigone did not dwell beyond recognizing its truth and trying to placate her sons' wives.

Deborah de Courcy's arrival allowed Antigone to once more speak English. With the baby on either lap at different times, the two women constantly chatted about England and what it meant to them. The ranch hands began shirking their jobs for lack of attention as Antigone devoted so much time to her granddaughter. Before Alexandra's arrival, Antigone was known for her sharp stings of rebuke at finding some slackness. Basking in her granddaughter's gurgles of smiles, she remained anchored to the main house.

When the sun shined, the two women could be seen pushing Alexandra's baby carriage and having three-way conversations with a baby who comprehended little but the attention given. Lurking always in the background was the Duena, who approved of nothing she did not originate but was pleased with the attention given by the two women.

Knowing this idyllic interlude would pass, both women harbored secret dreads. After finding such an amenable companion in Deborah, Antigone's unsaid worry was losing both Alexandra and Deborah Her clouded past and uncertain future worried Deborah. Both fears were heightened when two Englishmen arrived. Explaining they were protecting Deborah but declining to say from whom this protection was needed, the men set up their equipment in one side bedroom, so they covered the hallway leading from the main entrance.

Aside from taking meals with the staff in the kitchen, the men did little to interact with others. When asked to join the ladies for lunch or dinner, they acquiesced but shared little insights about their reason for being there.

Two weeks into their assignment, Gertie showed up at the ranch with Enrique.

"It's time you left," she said to Deborah.

"But where will I go."

"To America with Enrique."

"But the embassy has my passport."

"I have your new passport here." Then handed her the coveted green-covered document.

"But it is in the name of Deborah Williams." Deborah replied after scanning the document. It appeared old and had numerous travel stamps from other countries.

"That's your new name. There is even a birth certificate to attest to your right to it at Somerset house.

"But why America?"

"Because Enrique says your good for Alexandra and they need an English nanny to keep their promise to their son-in-law."

"There will be a lot of English speakers in America."

"Enrique wants his granddaughter speaking as if she came from Buckingham Palace."

"We can do that but what about Vittorio?"

"Who?" Gertie said with a meaningful look at Deborah.

Understanding the message, she switched to ensuing events.

"When are we leaving?"

"Tonight. The sooner the better and you'll go west through Colombia."

"There will be a plane waiting to take Enrique, the baby, that native woman and you to Barranquilla. From there to Jamaica through to Tampa. You'll go by train the rest of the way to Washington."

"Where will we live?"

"Washington if I guess right. Enrique bought a home for his daughter."

"Antigone will be so sad at losing her granddaughter."

"She has other grandchildren."

"For some reason this one is special. I suppose we all have favorites."

"Having favorites can sometimes hurt you," Eleanor said, looking away from Deborah and the distant hills.

Crying fiercely at the parting foisted on her, Antigone acted quickly, readying the child and her nurse for the journey. Enrique hurried them through the preparations, not being overly verbose, newly arrived suddenly from the city, finally bundling them into his big Buick in the early afternoon. About to leave, he hugged his wife, and the embrace was the closest they came to intimacy since Christiana's conception. With two Venezuelan policemen as outriders, their caravan headed to the border. No one looked back, and Alexandra slept.

The two men grabbed some sleep back at the ranch before setting up a vigil facing the long corridor leading to the main living area.

Gertie slept too but woke just as the sunset. She sat in a big chair, waiting for whoever was coming to find Deborah. She had done her job, and now it was up to her to end this enemy's career. It was her task to complete it at the ranch.

# March, 1941
## Christiana and Eric Dykman

Neither was America ready for the coming war nor Washington society prepared for Christiana. Of the two, society matrons in general and the young men in the diplomatic corps adjusted quicker and better.

While Washington society made room for newcomers, the nation's military ignored lessons being painfully learned by the belligerent powers. Especially when it came to supplying far-flung military and civilian populations. For instance, how dependent the German army was on horses. When the Germans invaded Russia, the Communist regime had five times as many tanks as the Wehrmacht. The American military was trading its horses for tanks but not at a pace to enable it to fight the coming conflict.

Despite the proven ascent of airpower, Washington naval leaders still assumed the war would be won or lost in one titanic big-gun, fleet-to-fleet engagement. Their faith was in the orange war plan refined during the 1930s, which relied on the US fleet advancing west in the Pacific to an all-out engagement with the Japanese home forces. All expected a short war, not the long-slog World War II ultimately became. Under this scenario, the war planners did not believe naval airpower and superior production capability would ultimately decide the victors.

Of minor importance to the nation but vital to its participants, Washington society believed the city would remain the center of the universe with acceptance decided by birth rather than wealth or political power. While the coming war ultimately shredded these barriers, younger pre-war generation members also played a role. Starting with the roaring Twenties and the upheavals of the depression, newcomers' new blood changed society in the nation's capital.

One center of change was the South American embassies. As Washington became the most desired foreign posting, embassies were staffed by two groups—those that played and those that worked.

Fueled by the demographic evolution in South America, embassies became work centers instead of social centers. This change led to splits in staff make-up.

Hoping to avoid dynastic inheritance battles, many wealthy, elite families used their country's diplomatic service to prevent friction among male siblings. By pushing overseas diplomatic assignments for second and third-born sons, the expectation implicit in the arrangement was that the younger siblings would find new careers and/or wives and remain overseas and not return home to challenge the eldest and principal heir. In many cases, the ploy worked. For others stronger in character, scions returned to their native countries unhappy with secondary roles demanding some part of the family riches. This dynamic led to continued turmoil as succession often proved difficult if not impossible without significant upheaval. Many dynasties faltered when the latter outcome prevailed.

In the Washington diplomatic scene, many of these rich men in their twenties eschewed the mundane tasks required of embassy clerks. Such duties fell to career diplomats, often from their country's emerging middle class The division between staff workers and dilettantes led to animosity and unhappiness not noticed by the elites until it boiled over into hostilities.

That is not to say some of these sons became valuable professional diplomats. However, in embassy after embassy through the pre-war and conflict years, the enmity grew, leading to many post-war problems. These disaffected individuals became rich fodder to be suborned by communist and CIA operatives in the post-war period devoted to fighting Russian-inspired penetration in the Western Hemisphere.

Sensing the changes coming and feeling the impending change affecting their privileges during the last years of peace in Washington, a sub-culture of wealthy South Americans made an art of partying. Naturally, knowing of her escapades as a teenager, she was invited to join them in their hedonistic partying once this crowd learned of Christiana's presence. The myriad invitations offered a heady series of parties, outings, and drunken revels that quickly threatened her home life.

Unfortunately, at this time, Eric was away almost constantly. His absence left Christiana lonelier than she had ever been. Even her family's presence was not enough. Between the Duenas and Deborah DeCourcy, her duties as a mother and mistress of the house were minimized. Socially, she still was fecklessly flirtatious. In her loneliness, Christiana suffered the company of the young men and their mostly American socialites who reveled in the last days and nights in a Washington about to change forever.

Eric did not like being away but knew what he was doing was important. Based on his South American experience, he was detailed to evaluate America's capacity to provide support to its troops should they be required in the future. What Eric found dismayed him.

Despite massive Allied purchases of foodstuffs, guns, equipment, cars, and trucks in a rapidly rearming American industrial complex, getting them to the warring countries presented problems. Moving these cargoes to East or West Coast ports was not done efficiently or in ways to allow the railroads to prepare for even greater transporting needs in the future. Unless better methods were learned and deployed, Eric feared the anticipated war production would lead to chaos getting these supplies to the war zones.

His South American experience proved that current ship loading and dispatching was haphazard and dangerous. There was no effective means of coordinating departures to protect the ships once they left port. Vessels departing American harbors could be easily torpedoed by German U-boats before they ventured 50 miles. Still, like many other officers in Washington, Eric realized that many changes were needed when war came. His worry and eventually his responsibility was whether America could sustain an overseas combat force.

At Admiral King's direction, Eric was assigned to the Navy's supply department. Again, the CNO directed that he be tasked with evaluating each port, the docks, labor situation, and security.

With the orders came copies of his report on South American shipping efforts. Unfortunately, it was not read by senior staff members charged with moving supplies who resented the young officer's intrusion into their domain. Assigned a small office and no help, Eric was unaware of the snub in his space assignment or cognizant that his promotion to Captain was quietly shelved by noting lack of sea duty.

Eric started a methodical review of American harbor establishments, ignoring the slights and giving priority status to travel where and when he wanted. What he found troubled him In port-after-port, Eric was stung by how unprepared and the lack of security permeated senior admirals. Given his South American experience and brush with death, this latter point particularly concerned him.

Even naval installations proved to be inadequate for the conflict ahead. Worse, from Eric's point of view, the naval supply command was not concerned about the possible dearth of transportation or the ability to supply troops in a two-ocean war.

Returning from each port visit, Eric wrote up his observations and submitted them up the chain of command. Often, he heard nothing but to be given further orders to review another facility. Again, Admiral King's orders conflicted with the Supply Command, who wanted nothing to do with the brash officer.

For the first time in his life, being away from home gnawed at him. Alexandra was growing, and each time she ran to him upon his return tugged at his heart. Since his journeys were often spur-of-moment, as was his return, sometimes Christiana was not there. Always, she rushed home the minute he appeared, and she would find him playing with their daughter.

In a flush of heat and longing, she demanded he immediately join her in their aerie despite his desire to continue interacting with his daughter. By the time they finished, Alexandra was asleep, her newest gift from Eric wrapped in her arms. Once, he put his foot down to stay with their daughter on such an occasion. Christiana pouted but then joined them on the floor, joyously embracing them both.

# April, 1941
## Rick Huntington

Eric Dykman was worried about how his wife would adjust to Washington. In reality, he worried about how Washington would react to Christiana.

Not everyone's cup of tea, as he well knew, she was uniquely herself. His natural reticence did not encourage intimacies. As a consequence, he had few intimate friends. On the other hand, his wife was a person who attracted others like a light to moths.

One close friend was Commander Rick Huntington, whose wife was the epitome of naval wives. She was dedicated to his career but could carve out a place of her own. How she and Christiana would get along, he did not know.

At dinner that night, Rick looked across the table at his wife, Marvel. Still, as trim as the night, he first saw her in a mixer for midshipmen and eligible girls from colleges such as hers, Martha Washington. From Nashville, Marvel Honeycutt Scofield came from a long line of American soldiers and sailors. All ranking officers, either generals or admirals. Like Christiana, Marvel decided who she would marry upon first seeing the man. A decision unshared until Marvel revealed it to Rick years later.

Marvel's well-organized campaign got her what she wanted, an Annapolis wedding coupled with an East Coast ship posting. Rick learned he had someone dedicated to one goal from the moment they were married. Setting her cap to be an admiral's wife, she did everything to achieve that rank.

But tonight, there was a different agenda. As the two couples made their way into the Congressional Hotel's dining room, soft music from the band was playing in the background. Seated at their table, the two women eyed each other. The men looked on apprehensively. Like two tigers circling in a cage, the women exchanged notes, ignoring their husbands.

After two drinks, their talk got looser, relaxing everyone at the table. When Christiana ordered another drink, Marvel added to her order. After the third drink was consumed, Marvel demanded her fourth. Christiana followed suit, each wife looking at the other. Another round followed for the two women. The husbands wisely declined refills. Acting as observers, the two officers were ready to carry their wives out discreetly as the women drank their fifth, sixth, and seventh rounds.

Rick knew his Tennessee-born wife could hold her liquor but had never seen her be a challenged drinker.

Secretly smiling, Eric had heard of the near-legendary feats of drinking Christiana had accomplished growing up. Since their marriage, she had almost totally quit. He wanted to intervene but knew this was an important test for both women. Despite the flow of liquor, neither woman showed signs of drunkenness. When another round was ordered, both men became concerned. Reverting to calling Eric by his academy nickname, Rick asked Eric to collect the check before another round could be signaled, and both women broke out in laughter.

"Christiana we are going to be great friends," Marvel said brightly.

"Marvel, you bet you! Christiana replied and burped.

"No one can outdrink me."

"I just did."

"No, I had two before we met because I was nervous."

"So did I," Marvel screamed, hugging the other woman.

Indeed, even though 10 years separated the ages of the two women, they were the best of friends until Christiana's death. Often tooling around Washington in Christiana's yellow Buick, they shared many a drink and incident. What always struck Marvel was Christiana's ability to flirt with any man from 18 to 80 and leave him without stirring animosity.

Another was Christiana's love for Eric. His duties kept him away for days on end, and she would be out and about helping others, caring for her daughter, and working at the Red Cross. But the minute she knew her husband was coming home, she ran to make sure she was there to meet him.

There was never any doubt in Marvel's mind of Christiana's love for Eric or his for her. The age difference, the cultural disparities, and even her wealth did not come between the couple. Quite by accident, Marvel learned just how wealthy Christiana was and how much more she would receive on her 25th Birthday. Marvel and Christiana quickly became best friends. She was a bit jealous but also glad for her friend. Marvel wondered if heartache ever would touch her.

One other thing came out of that night: Christiana heard Eric's nickname for the first time. Afterward, she called him and referred to him as "Nestor."

# March, 1941
## Sven Bernadotte

Dust swirled around his black limousine, further obscuring the dark, unlit road ahead. Combined, the two factors forced Sven Bernadotte's driver to slow down at almost every curve or as they passed through darkened towns.

Because the Venezuelan plains south of Caracas were sparsely settled, like the roar of a malevolent beast, the machine's engine's noise woke many settlement residents as it raced through the main street. Worried some resident would call ahead, announcing his progress did not please the German spy and two hand-picked killers.

Along the way, they cut the telephone wires to ensure no advance word reached Antigone's ranch. He had solved the vexing puzzle of Vittorio Massaro's disappearance, and now it was time to confirm the details and exact vengeance.

Months of fruitless searching and inquiries for the Italian spy or English embassy lady finally yielded the news of her supposed ranch stay. Assuming Massaro was dead was easy. Still unsure of the exact cause of Massaro's fate, Sven and the Italian embassy wanted details they thought only the English lady could give.

Not trusting the Italians to do this vital job properly, Sven undertook the task himself. Seeing the nature of what was to be done, he was forced to ask his Berlin masters for support. Pleased with the diplomatic code coup, they agreed, warning him to avoid trouble if possible.

Thinking they might say the information was not worth the potential damages to other operations, Sven knew if informed some killing was possible, they might cancel the attempt, so he did not provide all the details to Berlin.

Unlike his two companions, who were attached to the embassy and enjoyed diplomatic immunity, Sven faced legal consequences if anything went wrong. Therefore, he prepared carefully for this night.

Paying an informant for a plan of the house and staffing routines, Sven was reasonably sure the three men could handle any opposition at the ranch. Its remote location, long history of peaceful existence, and small staff portended little or no trouble.

Sven was confident of success, assuming that the pre-dawn descent on the ranch would neutralize any opposition with heavy armaments and his ruthless willingness to kill. Their plan was to carry off the woman for interrogation later. Alternatively, they would kill her there and thus tie up a loose end to the embassy affair.

Arriving at the ranch with the 4'oclock hour, the men left the car outside the fenced garden and made their way quietly to the front door. Unlocked but closed against the mosquitos, the men tossed beef to the three-guard dogs stirred by their activity. Wolfing the offering down, the dogs circled the intruders in hopes of more treats. No barks emanated from them nor any other sounds from inside the house.

The Germans advanced inside the front room, which served as an office and reception space, emboldened by the silence. Following the diagram given by their informant, they started down the long hallway leading to the living quarters. Sven was in the rear, preceded by his two burly companions.

When all three were in the passageway, lights suddenly brightened the area revealing two men with drawn guns facing them, cutting off access to the living quarters. Trained as they were, the two henchmen immediately opened fire with the heavy machine guns they carried. Their burst cut down one of the blocking figures but not before his weapon and that of the other man tore into them both.

Protected by his companions' bodies, Sven retreated to the reception room only to be met with bullets from someone firing a lighter caliber pistol. He fired twice towards the flashes and managed to reach the door. Having only an automatic with six rounds left, he traversed left to right, looking for his assailant. Seeing nobody, ran out the door through the lawn to his car. One more burst of automatic fire from one companion's gun, then silence inside the house.

Reaching the car, Sven fumbled with the starter sequence but managed to coax the engine to life. Prepositioned to leave quickly, he turned not back to Caracas but south and west to Colombia. He stopped to cut the telephone wire a mile away and headed for the border.

Reaching the bustling town of San Cristóbal Táchira, Sven abandoned the car in an apparent lawless area of the city, hoping it would be stolen or stripped. He strolled the streets until stealing another vehicle parked inside street share. Hours later, Sven was at a Colombian customs station displaying the spare passport the agent carried at times. Perhaps having an inkling about this caper, he'd sewn it into his jacket lining with currency from three different countries before leaving Caracas.

With the guard's curtsy wave, Bernadotte, posing as Piet Nordstrom, passed through the flimsy border checkpoint and headed to Bogota. In the next commercial hub, Cucuta, he abandoned the car for the rickety bus and train service. He was tired from his travels but still wary. Later that night, Sven approached the German chauffer in Bogota at the whorehouse frequented by staff. After verifying each other by exchanging coded phases, Sven was sneaked into the embassy at night. There, for the first time in days, he slept well. Sven was depressed by the mission's failure and angry at the realization that he was duped.

Vowing vengeance, he cabled Berlin for orders. Pleased one of their best operatives was safe, they ordered him to Manaus, the key transshipping center for much of the Amazon basin. The task was the first of many assignments given to Piet Nordstrom nee Sven Bernadotte. In all cases, the directive involved getting vital supplies to the Axis powers while at the same time denying resources to the Allies.

Sometimes successful, sometimes thwarted, he played a significant role in the wartime conflict waged in civilian clothes by operatives on both sides. Despite the German operative's best efforts, once cargoes left the continent, the British and American navies' sweep of ocean trade ultimately prevented many supplies from reaching Germany.

While successful in naval interdiction, Piet's success at sabotage, murder, intimidation, and delay reached a level requiring some focused response from the allied intelligence agencies. In late 1943 they put a $50,000 bounty for his capture or death.

Upon hearing the reward, an angry Piet killed the British agent in charge of their Porto de Santo establishment. Out of the country, when the deed was accomplished, his bounty was raised to $100,000 and changed to death. Realizing the danger this put his other operatives, he received Berlin's permission to relocate to Bogota and find a new identity. As 1944 opened, Piet was once again trading Swedish domestic products. Laughing to himself, he realized the irony of coming full circle back to selling rather than spying. If he thought his spying days were over, he was mistaken.

# May, 1941
## Enrique De la Vega

Spring came late to Washington, as did the de la Vega entourage. Held in Peru by red tape, Alexandra's fever, and fear of German reprisals, the group completed the long trek in autos supplied by the Venezuelan Ambassador. Drawing up in front of the Dupont Circle residence, they expressed their relief differently. Alexandra leaped from the arms of her Duenas into Eric's chest. Her daughterly ties were not forgotten during her travels. Enrique quietly embraced his daughter. The Duenas and Deborah DeCourcy stood patiently by as the family reunited.

With little baggage but much hope that day, the seven individuals divided up the house in the manner it remained for years. The father took the first and second floors, and the two retainers occupied the third floor, with Alexandra at the top level reserved for Christiana and Eric. Before her family arrived, Christiana installed a bathroom and small kitchen on each of the floors, making them all separate units.

She did not realize how prescient this became when her two brothers, sisters-in-law, three nephews, and niece suddenly appeared at the end of the summer. They were informed the two males were targets of a Caracas assassination attempt to their collective dismay. Not having been told of the ranch attack or the real reasons for their father's hasty flight to America, they had come to the capitol for explanations.

Unsure of what to tell his sons, Enrique prevaricated while seeking Eric's input. Unfortunately, their arrival coincided with his trip to southern ports to identify their individual shipping capacity. The days waiting for his return added to the boys' discomfort and provoked animosity between father and sons. When he did return, Eric's counsel was to urge truthfulness.

As they sat down in his apartment to lay out all the details, the Venezuelan Ambassador arrived with terrifying news. He reported two men invaded the ranch and shot Antigone, killed two men assigned to guard her, and were caught fleeing the property. With their mother in critical condition, the sons left immediately for Caracas, leaving their families behind.

They were too late. Antigone died two days after the incident. Her assailants claimed diplomatic immunity from the Italian Embassy and boarded a ship for Naples before the sons reached Venezuela. As these events unfolded, there was much grief in the home. The sons turned on their father in their anger, blaming him for their mother's death. In reality, Enrique also felt responsible. No one felt more keenly about Antigone's death than Deborah DeCourcy. Events could be traced directly to Antigone's offer of sanctuary to the English woman, and it was a burden she felt for the rest of her life.

Although somewhat estranged or at the least separated, Enrique was stunned by Antigone's death. Despite living apart and the presence of multiple mistresses, she was his anchor throughout his marriage, the only woman he truly loved. Her death hit him very hard. Worse was the rejection his sons were exhibiting towards him, and they heavily insinuated that he did not return for the funeral.

Nor interestingly did they want their families to rejoin them. Questioning their attitude, the wives sensed that fear for their safety was uppermost in the sons' minds. Enrique thought they wanted to be free of their wives' oversight yet claim marital status should some over amorous woman want more than a nighttime stand.

As world hostilities drew America further into combat situations, so also were the conflicts between father and sons. With Enrique in America, effective control of their companies devolved on their shoulders.

When Antigone's will was read, the sons were surprised to find Alexandra received the bulk of her estate, including her home in England held in trust through Eric. To satisfy Venezuelan law, there were bequests to her other living grandchildren but noted they were heirs to the sons' shares of the company. Enrique received nothing except her portrait painted when they were married and 1000 Venezuelan Bolivars.

A codicil written just days before her death gave Deborah the equivalent of $10,000 to start a new life. There was also a requirement of a lifetime pension for the Duenas. This sinecure to begin at any point the older woman chose along with a necklace she had long admired. This last point was never honored as the sons refused to give him the jewelry their mother had in her possession when she died.

Disheartened by his wife's death and realizing his grandchildren were destined to remain in America for some time, Enrique agreed to sell his companies to them. After much haggling and lawyerly expenses, the transfers were affected by Thanksgiving 1941. Enrique had secured his American investments and assured Christiana of her wealth. Enrique was comfortably surrounded by his grandchildren while not as rich as when he first arrived.

When the house next door was put up for sale, he swooped in and purchased it for his two daughters-in-law. They divided the house and granted his wish to use the basement as a workshop.

Christmas 1941 was a joyous occasion in the two homes despite the war's beginning. No one realized it would be the last family Christmas for years.

# November, 1940
## Miriam Brinkerman

The period in England between the two world wars has been called the Long Weekend. War was a frightful subject not to be discussed to young English aristocrats of this period, many of whom were too young to be slaughtered on the Western front or not yet born to the survivors and avoiders.

Seared by their parents' agonies or frightened at the prospect of fighting for what they perceived as a collapsing empire, many sought refuges as pacifists or communists. Some devoted their energies to recapturing the nation's Victorian-inspired optimism by creating echoes of the past, including restoring older homes and manors.

In picturing these efforts as the long weekend often mentioned are the English country house parties held weekly until the second and most agonizing conflict began. While restricted to only the most socially connected, entry to these parties and other events was necessary if one wanted to join the social elites.

Because this caste system was straining to stay as insular as possible, new entrants faced difficult hurdles to acceptance. Most social climbers failed in their goals. The few that did succeed became "more English than the English." As one writer described these social climbers who participated in this time and its populace. Those who did best were very rich, power brokers and creators of bold material displays. One constant among them was that they tried to please those they thought above them. Wartime service and also a bestowed title didn't hurt. Once they became the elite of the elite, in an ironic turn, they also became the most snobbish, looking down at those that came after them.

One way of gaining entry was purchasing or leasing a country estate, the more extensive with the highest pedigree, the better. This requirement also acted to put roadblocks in the way of the most determined and richest. Concurrent with the demand for estates was the need for personnel to run them.

Country manors needed men and women to keep them in repair and operating. Their upkeep did not diminish with the first war's end, and neither did the farms whose produce earned the monies for all other activities. What changed were the people on the estates. World War I forever broke the farm-to-manor link. Freeing tenants from the manor forever. A shortage of laborers turned many large estates into albatrosses requiring more management skills than their noble lords possessed.

Another final blow to the English countryside was the death duties imposed during and after the wars and never rescinded. Their enactment was the final blow to the old order.

In the twilight time of 1938, Miriam Brinkerman went to Cambridge to study literature. She inherited blue eyes and light brown hair from her pure German grandparent. From her father's mother's full breasts and long legs with a tapered backside. Jewish men and women were described as "exotic" or "Semitic looking in the country house set." This description was not ascribed to her. In fact, after seeing her in a bathing costume, one admiring baron described her as "a Nordic goddess."

Deliberately when applying to Cambridge, she used her grandmother's surname, Graf Holstein. Entry into the country house set was relatively easy between her brains and attractiveness. Soon she was enjoying weekends at elite estates and manor houses. When queried who her people were, she indicated they were in shipping, usually managing to turn the conversation away. It was enough for hostesses to know of her friendship with this Earl or that Count. As the nation entered 1939, Miriam was happy at school and socially.

A telegram from home messaged her brother's death. Not revealed until she returned home, he died bringing guns into Palestine. Knowing how keenly her father would feel the loss, she went to sit Shiva only to find there was no outward recognition of his loss. Her father, not wanting to bring too much attention to his son's activities, put about that he had gone to America. Seeing her perplexity, it was at this time Miriam was apprised of just how deeply her father was committed to the Zionist cause.

Still taken with her social whirl, Miriam went back to Cambridge and the life she thought she wanted. When war came, she was just 20. Initially swept up in the patriotic fever, Miriam wanted to join. When many of her friends from the university held back, it took her up short. Three girlfriends and four members of the aristocracy even went on peace marches. She did not want to take sides, but remained friendly with those for and against the war effort. As the "Phony War" dragged on, like many of her fellow students, she continued her studies, completing her second year with encouragement from the professors for the following terms.

Going home after exams, her father talked with her about joining the war effort.

"Things are bad in Germany and they will get worse for us," he said.

"We are safe her, Papa," she rejoined.

"But what if England loses?"

"That will not happen."

"We said it would not happen in Germany but it has."

"You don't believe those propaganda stories."

"We have letters. We know people who have escaped."

"But what can we do, Papa?"

"We will never be safe until we have our own homeland again."

"Papa, that is the world of your dreams."

"I may not see it but I pray you will."

"England is my homeland."

"No, you will see they will only tolerate us. We need our own homeland."

"Papa, you are wrong."

"No, time will show you I am right."

They spoke no more about his hopes, but she joined a civilian women's group just in time to see the defeated British army return from Dunkirk beaches. Throughout the summer, she was involved in preparing the nation for invasion. When it was time for her to return to Cambridge in September, the German air raid blitz started. She stayed home, not wanting to desert her comrades in the auxiliary unit.

Wanting to do more but unsure how Miriam went to see Henry Batterson, someone she knew from her weekends in the country.

Actually, Earl of Northumberland, Henry was just nine when he inherited the title from his father, killed in the last months of World War I. As he was growing up, his mother constantly worried about his health, sports, activities, and friends in that order.

Henry was the last of his line, with no uncles, cousins, or even bastards to carry on the name. His mother's fear was the end of the family line, for she was, in her mind, the keeper of the flame for a family rooted in the 15th Century. This obsession turned into the dominating doyen of the estate and son.

Against his domineering mother, Henry's one act of defiance was choosing his father's profession for a career. Through his years at Sandhurst and first postings, his mother feared some accident, bullet, or sickness would kill him. She acted against his will, getting him a safe, non-combat billet.

When war came, Henry was an aide to the head of materials command, stockpiling food, weapons, and construction materials against the coming German invasion.

Knowing it was futile to fight his mother, Henry accepted his fate. He was almost glad at not being forced to determine if he had his father's courage.

When Miriam called, he invited her for drinks at the Savoy Hotel. He noticed how the men eyed her walking through the lobby when she arrived. Seated, they exchanged pleasantries and news of mutual friends. Finally, she asked him for help in being posted to some spot where her efforts would better contribute to the war efforts.

"It's no fun picking debris and finding bodies," she exasperatedly.

"Somebody needs to do it," he said with half a smile.

"But I think there is more I can do."

"Can you type?"

"I don't want to be a secretary."

"Wasn't thinking that."

"What are you thinking."

"We need help in my nick."

"Doing what."

"Can't tell you till your onboard."

"Why me?"

"Because you're smart. Pick up things. You're a diplomat? And you're easy on the eye."

"Let's not go into that again, Henry."

"Oh, don't worry about that. I've sorted out. Mum won't like it. But I feel better."

"I'm happy for you."

"Then you'll come with us."

"Is it better than picking up bodies."

"Worse, you'll be dealing with people who'll be squealing like neutered pigs."

"Then let's make them howl."

They clinked glasses, and the following week Miriam joined the Materials Command.

# September, 1941
## Deborah DeCourcy

Guilt as an emotion is magnified when experienced amidst other people in the dark corners of one's mind. Deborah DeCourcy's sadness continued long after the tragic events in Venezuela. Adding to her confusion was Antigone's understanding of her penniless plight. Unbeknown to Deborah, the dead women's will included a $10,000 bequest. Together, these two acts of kindness, offering her refuge and providing for her future, left Deborah's heart in pieces. This kindness continued as she remained part of a busy household where no one blamed her for the havoc at the ranch,

Vowing to pour Antigone's love into Alexandra, the Englishwoman added an extra layer of warmth to the baby's upbringing. As winter turned into the spring of 1941, Alexandra and her English tutor were inseparable. So much was the bond growing between them. Both Christiana and the Duenas felt more and more excluded. Tensions rose in the household, and only Enrique's quiet mediations tamped down the simmering anger.

Oblivious to the cross-currents, Eric was pleased with his daughter's growing fluency, albeit with an English accent. Deborah was everything and more he could hope in a tutor. So much was the improvement Christiana began speaking primarily in English to keep up with her husband and daughter. For her part, Alexandra enjoyed the attention coming from all sides of her household.

In the months after Antigone's death, Enrique, too, suffered great sadness. He remonstrated to himself for not spending more time with Antigone. Their sons did not help matters charging him with neglect of her, the business, and most importantly, resentment of his mentoring while they were growing up. He had no excuses for the first and third, blaming it on the need to devote energies to their financial well-being.

The sons considered him a failure in this area as well. They blamed Enrique for creating such a hodge-podge of businesses that they were hard-pressed to keep them profitable.

Like many scions, they thought of better ways to deploy their capital. Far away in Washington, he could not be close to events in Caracas. As hostilities broadened, Venezuela was gearing up for war with skyrocketing oil, meat, and food-stuff orders. The budding commerce was putting strains on the country's financial system. Thanks to Enrique's foresight in working with National City Bank, the sons had access to capital. How they used these funds worried him. However, recognizing their need to lead his enterprises, Enrique allowed them to buy his shares for a tenth of their value.

Sadly, the father also saw the sons had little interest in bringing their wives and children back to Venezuela. Neither did the wives seek to reunite with their husbands. Individually and then together, they informed him they would prefer to stay in the states.

Secretly pleased to have all his grandchildren so close, Enrique persuaded his sons to provide large trusts for their children and wives administered by him. After that, communications between father and his sons became less frequent. Eventually, all of the grandchildren became American citizens.

# December, 1941
## Miriam Brinkman

Despite the string of defeats suffered so quickly after America's entry into the war, most military leaders were confident of eventual victory. Spontaneous Christmas parties broke out in ministry offices, depots, armed forces camps, and ships.

Henry Batterson, Earl of Northumberland, raided the cellars in his baronial estate to offer passers-by drinks and dainties in the week before Christmas. Henry planned to stay in his Bristol office to avoid his mother while other staff members scattered to their homes.

Miriam also stayed, not wanting to confront her father and his Zionist efforts.

Lost in the labyrinth of corridors was Flight Lieutenant Ian Harcourt recovering from wounds and briefly assigned to Materials Command. The wine Henry pushed in the officer's direction sloshed onto his immaculate uniform.

"Sorry chappie," Henry said without the slightest bit of embossment.

"Nothing, just got it out of mothballs."

"You've not used it lately," queried Henry.

"Where we go a flight suit is better and been in hospital."

"Then you need something stronger. Miriam gets this man something stronger from my desk!"

Miriam stirred from her seat and walked into Henry's office with her back to the two men. Noticing the woman in civilian clothes for the first time, Ian's eyes followed her into the inner office. Despite Henry's continuing conversation, his eyes lingered at the door until she filled it again.

Miriam walked toward the two men with the scotch bottle in her hand, her eyes unfocused. Scooping up an empty glass from the serving table, Henry offered it to Miriam. It was at this point her gaze settled on the Flight Officer.

His smooth face betrayed signs of battle fatigue and the drain the injuries took from his body. Miriam uttered a single stuttered word and proceeded to pour the scotch onto his uniform, adding to the mess Henry created.

"I think I'm not wanted here," Ian said half-jokingly.

"No, no our fault really. Guess were not used to war heroes," said Henry.

"I'm no hero, just a pilot who can shoot straight."

"Those ribbons say differently."

"That's because I survived when others did not."

"I can't believe that," jumped in Miriam, able to speak now.

"Believe what you will but the medals mean little except you survived when the other fellows on your side and theirs didn't." Ian said somewhat bitterly.

Both listeners heard the sourness in Ian's voice and moved quickly to change the conversation.

"Who are you looking for?"

"Some chap named Symonds or Simson who's in charge of getting more silk for our parachutes."

"He's usually down the hall but gone until after Boxing Day," Henry mused.

"He can't be. The silk we have been getting is tearing, and we're losing men who bailout, and the chutes rip when deployed."

"That is scary," Miriam exclaimed heatedly.

"We need to do something and joining a party isn't my idea of doing something," Ian matched her anger.

"Indeed it's not. Miriam, you're detached to help Flight Officer Harcourt get to the bottom of this." Henry said, taking in the two of them.

"You can do that?" Ian asked.

"Just got promoted and in charge of the office so I can do anything. At least until the Brigadier returns and that won't be until next year. Miriam finds him better silk."

"Yes, sir," Miriam replied with more joy than she acknowledged to herself but not lost on Henry.

Steering Ian away from the party, the couple went to Symonds' office, whose only occupant was a burly one-armed Master Sergeant.

Apprised of Ian's mission, he said it was an RAF problem. Reminded in a nod to efficiency, his office was tasked with supplying silk for all branches, and the sergeant became doubly defensive. At this point, Miriam displayed the toughness and ability to find solutions learned at Henry's shoulder and was to characterize her life.

"Sargent, do you have the specs for parachutes?" She asked the tough veteran.

"Show them to me."

"I can't they're labeled secret."

"So what, we are here to learn why they're tearing when they're most needed."

"I can't show them without authorization."

"Well, I authorize you to do so."

"And who are you."

"I am the person that can get you transferred to northern Scotland or even a naval ship at Scapa Flow."

"You wouldn't dare. I lost my arm at Ypres and did my duty."

"Then do your duty now and get those specs."

The Sargent rummaged in the files, thoroughly cowed by the furious blond before him while the couple fidgeted in his office. Seldom at a loss for words, Miriam remained silent beside the quiet flying officer who seemed tightly wound and anxious. When the veteran returned, he had four thick files in his arms. They spread them out on a vacant desk, closely examining each sequentially by date. Two hours later, Miriam asked for copies of the latest purchase orders. After a brief demurral, he found invoices for the RAF's most recent order.

"The thread count requirement seems to have gone up in each set of specifications," Ian spoke first.

"I wouldn't know about that," said the soldier.

"Who would?"

"That would be Hastings."

"Who's Hastings?"

"He worked in this office until November when he was pensioned off."

"Who replaced Hastings."

"No one, we've been short staffed since then."

"So when a new order or spec comes in what happens?"

"We try to look at them to see if there is any change but most of the time we file them along with the previous specs."

"So if research or the field come up with something new or better or find the current equipment doesn't work it is up to your office to make the changes?" Miriam said with rising anger.

"That's the way it should work," the now visibly uncomfortable Sargent replied.

"For a year we have been complaining about the chutes and your office was supposed to fix that."

"You'll need to talk to Mr. Symonds about that," said the sergeant huffily.

Angry about what they had learned, Miriam and Ian returned to the now quiet offices where Henry was cleaning up.

"Come back to help, Miriam?" he said brightly.

"No, to dump a problem in your lap," she barked.

Motioning them into his office, they discussed the parachute situation in detail. Examining and discarding one solution saw Miriam and Ian become angrier and angrier. Midway through the impromptu meeting, Henry began laughing to himself. The angrier his two companions got, the closer they drew to each other. In the end, their legs and arms were almost touching to the apparent obliviousness of both.

Sensing there was more to the situation than neglect, Henry decided. While Miriam and Ian waited outside his closed door, the newly minted Colonel called a fellow peer in the War Ministry. As darkness fell, the three individuals who now felt companions in some sort of intrigue waited. After 6pm, the phone rang, and Henry listened to his instructions.

By tradition, civilians headed the procurement office, and given the perilous times putting a military officer in charge would raise issues. Taking Henry's advice, Miriam was named temporary head until an appropriate choice could be found. Symonds was called back to London from vacation to explain the parachute fiasco and anything else Miriam found. It was a very uncomfortable meeting leading to his sacking.

All this transpired before 9pm, double savings time. At this point, the three new friends realized they had not eaten anything for 12 hours.

The only place open was the rail station buffet, where they ate pastry pies and weak tea. Years later, Miriam would say it was one of the best meals.

When Henry discovered Ian had no lodgings and there was no transportation to his barracks, he invited the flyer home to his rented suite in a local hotel. Miriam went to her sparse room in a local bed-sitter, never expecting to see Ian again.

# December, 1941
## Henry Batterson,
## Earl of Northumberland

Bureaucrats of every nation fear scandal and shrink away even further from public knowledge of such malfeasance. Hearing from Henry how the Battle of Britain air heroes faced death from poor quality parachutes threw London ministries into panic mode. Smartly, Henry offered along with news of the impending catastrophe means of avoiding total exposure, and they went along with his suggestions

Two weeks before Christmas, Miriam found herself in Symonds' office examining every spec and invoice. A duo pulled from Henry's team found the pertinent material, but only Miriam read them. She reported back to him each night, painting a grimmer picture each day. Unsure of what he would do if informed, the ministries insisted Henry's boss be kept in the dark. No one yet knew the extent of the neglect or the identified fraud, which was even more worrisome.

On Christmas Eve, staff members were eager to be with their families, even if just for the two-day holiday period. Being Jewish, Miriam hadn't registered the anxieties of her two assistants until Henry breezed in to tell them their leave began at that moment.

Dismayed her help was deserting, Miriam remonstrated Henry. He just smiled and said she was coming home with him for the two-day holiday.

"No clothes," she pointed out.

"Mother has scads of newer nickers than she'll ever use."

"No presents, no clothes and no desire."

"You'll be here alone and that won't be good. Come home and enjoy my hearth and fire."

Realizing the invitation was more an order than a request, she forced him to stop by her room to hastily pack a small bag.

Henry's estate was close enough to Bristol that the darkened roads yielded a two-hour drive punctuated by three stops for security

104

checks. Miriam wondered how Henry got the gas for the big sedan meant more for a minister than a subaltern.

During the trip, Henry kept up a lively chatter avoiding all talk of the scandal they were slowly uncovering.

Before the war, Miriam guested at his estate and found it overwhelming in its grandeur. She also debated asking how it avoided being requisitioned as many other manors were for hospitals and evacuee children's hostels.

Anticipating her unasked question, he said in passing that sometimes it was used for hush-hush meetings or to debrief spies, emigres, and prisoners-of-war.

Driving up the long drive from the road to the house, Miriam surveyed the darkened windows and doused lights. Nothing showed on the hill upon which it was perched. The engine's roar must have alerted staff as the door opened quickly when they got out of the car.

Henry's mother opened the door and embraced her son with extraordinary warmth. She turned to Miriam and smiled with pleasure. They hurried inside, almost blinded by the room lights encased in heavy blackout curtains.

Marion, Henry's mother, could trace her ancestry back almost as far as his father. Whereas the father's family kept their lands and monies, hers did not. Her good fortune was to catch the 14th Earl's lustful look and parlay it into marriage, despite being almost penniless. In her mind, the land she held in trust for Henry until he reached majority. When he was of age, he chose to be a soldier, leaving the properties and investments to her management. Neither was dissatisfied with the arrangement.

Timing their arrival with the dinner hour, Miriam barely had time to go to her room and change into fresh stockings and dress before hurrying down to the table. The estate manager, his wife, the local minister, and Ian Harcourt were in the room when she entered. Blood rushed to her face when she saw Ian. He smiled, and Mariam looked at Henry's wide grin.

"Thought I'd give you the perfect Christmas gift," he said to her.

"Why would you think that?"

"By the look on your face now," he said happily.

"But how did you know?"

"When he left you that night, he kept me half the night talking about you. And do you know how much you talk about him?"

"No I never realized."

"You bring him in almost every conversation."

"Thank you so much."

"Don't thank me. Go over and give him a big hug. My mother says he has been in quite a state since he arrived this afternoon."

With that, Miriam rushed over and hugged the Flight Officer. At dinner, they sat next to each other oblivious to the other people at the table. Far from being put out, the other guests immensely enjoyed watching their halo of romance.

When the group adjourned for coffee and liquors, the two young people realized their neglect of the others. Not being able to talk about how they met or what was currently happening, the couple made up a story of meeting on the Bristol docks. It amused them, and Henry gave a romantic context to their relationship.

Henry and Marion's thoughtfulness extended to the holiday sleeping arrangements. Miriam and Ian discovered their rooms adjoined and connected by an inner door, turning in for the night. They did not come down for breakfast.

Henry's forethought extended to having matching heart-shaped pendants and chains engraved. Miriam's said simply "Ian," and his pendant was etched with her name. Miriam wore hers for the rest of her life.

Through Boxing Day 1941, the couple spent every moment together. Ian left first early in the morning following the holidays, and Miriam and Henry returned to Bristol and the widening scandal.

When finally, the Brigadier returned, Ministries requested he come to London immediately, and Henry was left in charge temporarily. The Brigadier never returned, and for the next year, Henry and Miriam managed to bring equipment purchased through the Bristol office in line with specs.

Because trials might attract public notice, none of the procurement officials or suppliers were ever charged. The original reason for the inquiry was that Parachutes were upgraded primarily by substituting nylon provided in abundance by America. Henry was promoted, jumping two ranks, and Miriam became his number one procurement officer.

Ian managed to see Miriam through March when he was reposted to his squadron.

This time as a flight leader. Wounded again, he was invalided an hour away by car from Bristol. Recovered, Ian once again joined his squadron after Christmas 1942. At Henry's insistence, Miriam and Ian spent that holiday with his mother and him. However, this time was not a happy time as Marion was dying of cancer, and she succumbed four days into the New Year.

Henry was inconsolable and requested a transfer to a combat unit immediately after her funeral. It was granted, and he joined the parachute corps after completing their rigorous training course in time to participate in Operation Market Garden. He was wounded in the abortive attempt to take the Anaheim Bridge and invalided out of the service. For the rest of his life, he lived at the manor. Mourning his mother and never marrying.

Knowing without his protection, Miriam would be subject to nasty reprisals from the civilian staff, who were vigorously questioned during the scandal investigation. Before leaving Bristol, Henry arranged for Miriam to be shifted to the American supply operation. He knew her skills would be needed for the coming D-day invasion.

# February, 1942

## Eric Dykman

Following the shock of Pearl Harbor, America geared up for war. Shipping rates soared as demands for transporting military and civilian goods strained the capacity of the nation's trucks, trains, and vessels. In three short months of conflict, the volume of goods moving through ports and depots up and down the East and Gulf coasts threatened to overwhelm their ability to move freight across the Atlantic. The situation was even worse on the West Coast and was only eased somewhat when military units took over many key shipping points.

Military leaders were advised to find a different solution on the East Coast. "Talk to the mob bosses and get some sort of agreement," was the suggestion of government criminal investigators advised quietly." They want something you may be able to give them."

The mob wanted the release of crime boss Charles "Lucky" Luciano, one of American history's most ruthless, engrammatic mobsters. In jail for pandering and other offenses, he maintained control of the docks through a series of henchmen.

None was higher or more ruthless than Anthony "Big Tony" Massucci. At age 50, Big Tony was the undisputed dock master in New York and top advisor to mob leaders who controlled other East Coast port cities. While these bosses claimed they answered to no one, they listened if Big Tony spoke in his quiet voice.

Besides his acumen in getting contracts for his men, Big Tony ran an efficient distribution network for the goods plundered during the loading and unloading of the breakbulk cargoes, then the norm in shipping. One in every 10 bottles of scotch flowing through the ports ended in Big Tony's distribution network. And that was only the tip of the operation.

Should muscle be required to straighten out any dissenter or shipper not wanting to play ball, Big Tony also supplied that. This came primarily in the form of Sal Vassallo. Deep-set eyes narrowed into slits when angry. His six-foot-four frame was solid muscle toned by two prison stretches, most of which were served in solitary confinement. Sal could accept a prison term but not be ordered by guards. Within weeks of arriving at a prison, his attacks on guards would guarantee he would serve the entire sentence in solitary.

When Sal arrived at a tavern or social event, things got quiet, and within minutes he would be the only person at the bar. Everyone knew he was liable to explode at any moment and preferred not to be around. Sal would agree with the general opinion that he was nuts in his few truly sane moments.

What saved him every time from being given a permanent exit was Big Tony. The mob leader protected Sal and got absolute loyalty from the madman in return. What holds Big Tony had on Sal was anyone's guess. Big Tony did not get his nickname from his stature or after becoming the important mob figure he was today at five foot two.

Armed with this intelligence, the Admiral in charge of East Coast shipping wondered who to send as an emissary to reach some accommodation during the war years. Chuckling to himself, he realized there was only one man who qualified.

"At ease Dykman," the Admiral said.

"You were pretty good at getting the South American stevedore gangs to cooperate. If I remember reading in your reports."

"We just found ways of being mutually beneficial to each other."

"Got a tougher nut for you to crack."

"I didn't speak their language."

"You still don't speak their language. This is the Dago longshoremen bosses on the East Coast."

"Heard you were having trouble. Why me?"

You've got docks working well in other parts of the world, why not here at home."

"Worth a try. What do I have to bargain with."

"Not much, I leave it up to you? I don't want to send in the Marines to run the ports. They're needed elsewhere."

"Wouldn't do much good. There's a thousand ways they can hold you up if they want to."

"Your job is to make them want to help not hinder."

Dressed as a civilian, Eric spent a week surveying operations in New York and Boston and talking to shippers, Coast Guard personnel, and even a few dock workers. Together with an FBI folder, he prepared to meet Big Tony. In civilian clothes permitting him to blend in more with the surroundings, Dykman chose the moment to introduce himself. At the same time, the man ate at his usual noontime haunt, *Victor's*, just behind police headquarters in lower Manhattan. Sliding in underneath a guard into the empty seat next to Big Tony. Just sitting down without being asked was enough to anger the crime boss. His bodyguards made moves to stop him, but they were signaled to back away.

"Mind if I ask you a question?" Eric opened his gambit.

"Why not? You've been asking questions all week," the mobster said with half a grin.

"I thought you might know I was around by now."

"Always like to know what is happening on my ground."

"You run a tight ship. No holes."

"Only way to stay afloat and not sink."

"But you can always use some help."

"Only if I'm in trouble. Am I in trouble?"

"Depends what you mean by trouble. Best to avoid any possibility of danger.

"So you know the land, you know my people, now you're here.

"So you want something in return for avoiding trouble."

"Yes, two things labor peace and smooth cargo handling with less pilfering."

"Tall order and why ask me?"

"Because you can help me accomplish all three and no one else can."

"Are you that sure about me?"

"We know it's true so let's get down to what you want and see if we can do something to get you what you want."

"The big guy out of prison."

"Can't happen until the war ends."

"Mass exemptions from military service for my men."

"No can do, Act of Congress needed. On a case-by-case basis maybe 100 or so."

"No investigations or indictments."

"On the federal level, yes, but we can't stop the states but we won't share information."

"Feds stop bothering us in other areas."

"Can't do and I want no pilfering from outbound military or military assistance cargos. The men overseas need everything they can get right now."

"Wouldn't have happened anyway. We're patriots here. You get me the guarantee on the Big Fella and you got a deal which will go for all the ports except Jacksonville, that one you will need to deal separately. They don't listen to me on anything."

"I'll be back to you. How do I reach you? No one seems to have your number."

"Here every Tuesday or Thursday. Call here other days and just say you need to talk to me. You have a card, don't you?"

"Yes, I do."

Eric went back to Washington and wrote up the memorandum that eventually was bucked up to the White House. After the deal was approved, officials in Washington kept the details secret, knowing the next New York Governor might be the man who convicted Big Fella. No news of the agreement was passed to the state where the pardoned would be executed.

Over the next six months, Eric became the liaison between Big Tony and the Navy Department, among his other tasks. Eventually, his work included other services as well. Big Tony tested the captain on deferments, investigations, and other matters. The two built up a working and personal relationship. So much so that Eric finally asked him about his nickname.

"Why the moniker Big Tony? Eric asked at one of their lunches at Victor's.

"Because I got a big one."

"Big one?" Eric said, puzzled.

"You know. I got a really big one that satisfies all the ladies."

"Oh," the listener finally knowledgeable.

"Yeah, no one wants to go take a leak with me because they get embarrassed."

"I see," Eric said, trying to change the subject.

"You know I got girls stashed all over the city. A chink in Chinatown. A society lady up town. One nigger in Harlem. And my wife in Red Hook. When I go home, she's out of commission for a week afterwards."

"I glad to see you so happy and making others happy."

"So, who's happy? These women cost dough and my time. Gotta keep 'em all happy. Wear's me out sometime."

"I'm sure," Eric said, bringing finality to the conversation.

It was a testament to the trust the two men had developed that in February 1943, Eric was invited to Big Tony's daughter's wedding at the Waldorf Astoria. The invitation began the events leading up to the tragedy of Eric's life.

# May, 1942
## Henry J. Kaiser

Increasingly, Eric's single-minded drive to improve the movement of war supplies across oceans encountered resistance from Naval and civilian managers charged with overseeing these operations. For many, his suggestions and outright orders went against established procedures, some of which dated from Clipper ship operations in the last century.

In one case, Eric noted cranes designed to off-load three tons at each turn were limited to half-ton pallets. When he asked why this limit, the longshoremen cited union rules. Working with Tony, Eric got this changed so loading could proceed at a faster pace.

In another instance, Eric observed tanks destined for Europe were not stowed below but spotted on the merchant ship's deck, making them vulnerable to being lost overboard in rough seas.

In both instances, the reasons behind decisions were based on old work rules and historical usage.

Angry that transit times in port and cargo space aboard vessels were being extended or under-utilized, Eric exploited his access to senior Naval officials to force through changes, thus adding ocean-going capacity and reducing time ships spent in port. Naturally, because they forced changes and sometimes dismissals, his successes aroused anger and some jealousy among those he worked with.

The highest among these antagonistic feelings were generated within the Navy's Sealift command. His successes brought about a series of personal and procedural changes that resulted in some old-line admirals being shifted or retired. This created a cadre of senior officers who devoted their efforts to retaliation toward him throughout his future career. Despite his many contributions to the war effort, they were able to use his lack of sea duty and other factors to delay his promotions. After the war, only exceptional circumstances and additions to his file kept him on active duty. Normally, under routine procedures, separation from the service rules forcing retirement loomed because he was passed over for promotion several times.

Particularly galling to many officers in the Bureau of Ships, was his opposition to the planned Liberty ships championed by that department and produced in large quantity by Henry J. Kaiser. The American millionaire, manufacturer, and life-long innovator proposed building one or two classes of merchant ships quickly using innovative building techniques.

As the war effort geared up, Kaiser developed innovative ways to turn untrained civilians into production workers. He was not the only one to do this but certainly one of the most active. Besides reaching out to women and teaching them to become welders, plumbers, and ironworkers, Kaiser proposed to build his ships in sections, turning them over so workers could weld downward. Learning to weld downward is relatively easy.

Under Kaiser's methods, as each ship's side was welded, the ship section was turned 90 degrees, enabling welders to continue.

Even before the war, when Britain ordered ships from American yards, Eric became interested in how the finished vessels could be more efficiently loaded and unloaded. He became more concerned when the basic design was adapted for the American Liberty ships. Two critical factors in their design worried him. These ships needed heavier cranes better positioned to more quickly in loading and unloading at a pier or off some beach. Also, he measured the hole openings and recognized many of the newer tanks and artillery pieces being developed would not fit given their larger footprint. Carrying them on deck would limit the number of armor Liberty ships could bring into combat zones.

After surreptitiously reviewing the blueprints, Eric voiced objections loud enough that senior admirals ordered him to meet with BuShips and Kaiser. Intrigued by what he heard about Eric, Kaiser asked for a dinner meeting, and they agreed to get together at the Congressional Hotel in Kaiser's suite early in December. When the builder said he was bringing his secretary, Eric invited Christiana along to make the meeting friendlier. Pleased she was finally joining Eric in his activities when the night arrived for the dinner, Christiana dressed demurely in a conservative blue dress.

A cab delivered them to the Congressional Hotel while daylight still lit the street. Moving through the hotel lobby amid the stares of the men as his wife passed by, Eric sighed, realizing no dress could hide his wife's figure. Eric noted the two burly guards at the elevator to Kaiser's suite floor. Another guard stood at the door. Two men in uniforms, their ranks hidden by their coats, departed as the couple arrived. The suite was spacious but strewn with papers, blueprints, empty cups, and briefcases. A smallish man given to bursts of energy; Kaiser was on the floor marking blueprints with a heavy wide pencil. A man hovered over him, taking notes. Another man was on the phone barking orders into the handset.

Kaiser turned when he saw the couple and got up.

"Who's this," he said harshly, motioning to Christiana.

"My wife, you said your secretary would be here, so I thought our meeting would be more sociable with women present."

"My secretary is Claude there in the corner. You think my wife would have me travel with a woman?"

"Stranger things have happened but I just assumed."

"You assumed wrong but hell, she's far more attractive than Claude. Let her stay."

"I don't think I want to Mr. Kaiser," Christiana spoke up for the first time.

"Don't get on your high horse Mrs. Dykman. Your husband's been causing me a lot of trouble."

"Well, I can cause you a lot more," Christiana said firmly.

"Please stay, when you hear what I have to say maybe your husband will stop bothering me."

"When you hear what he has to say maybe you'll change you plans whatever they are," she replied even more strongly.

"You have quite a filly there, Dykman," Kaiser said, a touch of envy in his voice.

"She's not horse Mr. Kaiser and maybe I think we should reconvene in the morning."

"By the morning I'll be gone. So, let's order dinner and you can tell me what's wrong with the ships I'm building."

With that, the atmosphere in the room relaxed a little, and the four people adjourned to the dining area. Drinks were produced, and a waiter was summoned. When he left, Eric grabbed up a profile drawing of a Liberty ship and explained why cranes with greater lift capacity needed to be added and repositioned because they would be necessary as newer, heavier equipment was introduced into the military. Eric pointed out alternative layouts when Kaiser talked about where weld points decided crane positioning.

Through dinner and over coffee Christiana and Claude were spectators as two men who were inveterate tinkers squared off about the building of what turned out to be 3000+ ships during the war. As the night wore on, each gained the respect of the other as the two men sought to build a better tool to supply the Allied cause.

Christiana stepped in to ease the tensions whenever the discussions started to get heated between Kaiser and Eric, using the wiles that tamed many men before them. By evening's end, changes to the design acceptable to both men were codified by Claude into a memorandum. He typed it before leaving with Kaiser and sent it to BuShips. Happy Kaiser had a thorn out of his side. BuShips accepted the changes incorporating them into many Liberty ships currently being built and all that followed.

The next day, Christiana received two dozen yellow roses from Kaiser. Claude remained with him throughout the war, never disclosing cancer eating his stomach. On VE Day, he died, and Kaiser paid for the funeral and put his two sons through college.

Kaiser tried to recruit Eric after the war, but he chose to stay in the Navy.

# May, 1943
## Christiana Dykman

More than one million men debarked for overseas assignments from the Brooklyn Marine Terminal during World War II. Almost all experienced ocean travel for the first time once their troopship passed the Sandy Hook lightship now dimmed against submarines. For most men waiting for their ships, barracks throughout the New York area served as their base for what leaves were granted. For patriotism and money, resourceful New Yorkers found ways to help these men cram as much as possible into their often-frenzied activities.

Hotels of quality and not-so-high standards ran nightly dances packed with servicemen and women, often married but alone. For the less adventurous, USO canteens and dance halls also offered relief from the anxiety many felt about their next posting. Given these crowded conditions, civilians who wanted to book weddings were often forced to accept dates months in the future if at all available.

Not for Big Tony to wait months when his daughter needed to marry in a hurry. He booked the grand ballroom at Brooklyn's St. Gorge Hotel. He accomplished the rapid engagement by convincing the head booker to reschedule two other events with a fistful of cash and a menacing glare.

Much sought by the mobster community and shipping executives, invitations to the event demonstrated positioning in the waterfront community. To his surprise, one invitation went to Eric Dykman, who received it with strong reservations. Slotted for the first weekend in May, he realized it coincided with Christiana's 25th birthday. Besides her upcoming birthday,

Eric was also wrestling with telling her of his new orders posting him to England. Requested by General Eisenhower's headquarters, he was being asked to look into improving the unloading of ships when they arrived in England. There was another aspect to the assignment which he would be told about upon arrival.

Since their marriage, he was often apart from Christiana but was always expected back. These orders meant separation for months, if not years. He was unsure how his wife would take their parting. Also, he was unsure how he would feel leaving the most exciting aspect of his life. Eric recognized his luck and the challenge of being Christiana's husband at his deepest levels. Never for her the easy path or the shying away from others. Often reckless in engaging strangers, Christiana always fell back on Eric to smooth any negative happenstance. His strength was her rock. It sustained her and enabled the escapades she was entertaining Washington society with at each occurrence. Most importantly, she would do anything to keep him.

A natural flirt, she ran through life unaware of how others felt until an event or person made her aware of some situation she caused to happen. Understandably, others took her words and actions as cues for their behavior towards her. Her friendliness and seeming ignorance of how beautiful she was encouraged men of all ages to mistake her motives. She, in turn, failed to see or willfully ignored the possible consequences of her actions. In a world where women were learning to be more openly flirtatious and seemingly more promiscuous, many men smitten by her could not believe how single-minded was her devotion to Eric.

His devotion to her was also overwhelming. Eric saw her vulnerability more clearly than she ever acknowledged to him or herself. He often chided her about the danger she courted. Once or twice, Eric talked to her about his fear that someone might take her friendliness for something more. There were men, Eric knew, who would not want to take no for an answer. She pood-pood the sentiment saying she enjoyed her exchanges with men and women.

Deciding to use the wedding to create alone time with Christiana, he first cleared their attendance with the Admiral nominally running his office. The Admiral, in turn, talked with navy intelligence, who conferred with the FBI. Finally, permission for Eric to attend was granted, but he was told not to wear his uniform. FBI surveillance teams assigned to cover the event were notified, and a memorandum was sent to FBI Director J. Edgar Hoover.

The report was added to the director's private file already being gathered on Eric. That Christiana deserved her own separate file was unknown until long after the war, and the bureau chose not to share it with local police in the subsequent investigation.

Then came the job of informing Christiana, who immediately said she was coming.

"We will make it our holiday," she said to him in bed.

"You don't know these people. What they expect." Pretending his resistance,

"It is a celebration. It is also my birthday weekend, we will celebrate."

On the first Friday in May, leaving Alexandra crying in Washington, the couple boarded the train to New York with happy hearts, both realizing this was the first time since their honeymoon that they would be truly alone.

While Eric toured the local docks, Christiana met Carlotta Ramirez, her schoolmate and teenage culprit-in-arms from Caracas now with the Venezuelan consulate. Laughing and giggling, the two old friends shopped for the dress Christiana felt she needed for the wedding. Four stores and numerous changes later, Christiana found the dress. At day's end, when Carlotta saw the room given to her friend, she used her diplomatic clout to get them a suite on the President's floor. This room came with a private butler, guarded access, and breakfast in bed. All things Christiana intended to use to the utmost. After the wedding, she wanted Eric for herself.

Despite wartime shortages, the wedding of Carmela Massucci included Maine lobsters, French champagne, assorted Italian pastries, and three wedding cakes. Fresh fruits were also there in abundance, but most disappeared into handbags and pockets to be brought home to children.

Traditionally, the wedding ceremony was sparsely attended, but Christiana chided Eric into going. Her long spring coat hid the yellow dress at the church, which was not revealed until they joined the cocktail hour back at the hotel.

Contrasting her dark skin, the off-the-shoulder dress highlighted her face and figure. Even Eric questioned why this woman chose him that day and remained enamored of this dour Yankee Naval officer. Seated near the head table, the couple enjoyed meeting their tablemates and listening to the band.

When the band played a soft, slow dance Eric took her to the dance floor. She cradled herself in his arm, enjoying the strength of his body. When a faster dance began, they began to walk off the floor. One of the more daring younger mobsters intervened and asked for her to join him. With a cock of her head, she swung smoothly into the number.

From then on, one man after another asked to be her partner. As Eric looked on, she rapidly attracted admirers while some of the other guests looked on, some of the women miffed at this inexhaustible woman.

As he admired her on the dance floor, Big Tony sidled up to Eric, watching his wife.

"You never said you had a young and beautiful wife."

"Men don't talk about their wives to other men where I come from."

"No, if she were my wife, I'd keep her in a convent."

"She wouldn't permit it. Pretty soon she'd have the nuns dancing."

"I bet she would. My compliments."

"Don't say that. Truth be known she picked me."

"I'll bet."

"Best thing ever happened to me."

"I'll agree with you there."

Christiana and Eric visited every table when the evening wore on and spoke with the bride and groom before leaving. Christiana found two antique vases to match their China set for their wedding gift. The bride appreciated the present, but the groom merely grunted.

As they left, men swarmed Christiana, throwing their goodbyes at her like petals. They did not notice Sal Vassallo sitting at his table alone, his tablemates deserting him as soon as possible.

The last person they saw was Big Tony.

"My dear, I could never imagine the captain here with a more different wife."

"What do you mean?"

"You are like a wildflower that waifs in the breeze."

"And you are a big man with the women. But my Nestor is rock on which we all stand."

"You call him Nestor and say he is a rock. Never heard either used for him."

"That is because few people know what a man he is. I knew it the first time I saw him."

Uncomfortable at being talked about in his presence, Eric broke in.

"Christiana, don't make more of me than I am."

"But I know who you are and so do others. I'm married to you forever."

"Man, you are hooked," Big Tony boomed jealously of the naked love displayed by the couple.

That night they made love and slept in each other arms, both realizing the power of that last exchange.

In the morning, they slept late, enjoying the warmth of each other. Not wanting to waste the spring-like day, Christiana jumped from the bed and ordered breakfast. As they waited, she raised herself on her knees to look at him.

You know I love calling you Nestor. You are so wise."

"Some people said I was dumb marrying you," he teased.

"And I you, but here we are. Are you happy?"

"With you yes. With the war. What I must do, no. But let us not talk about that now."

"Why, what must you do."

"Leave you. They want me to go to England."

"Poof I knew that. My friend Marvel told me. Her husband, your friend knew."

"You're not sad, angry?"

"Of course I am but they cannot win the war without my Nestor."

"Tell that to the generals."

"They already know that or they would not be asking for you."

"And here I was worried about telling you."

"I am a good Navy wife, no?"

"No, Christiana you will never be a good Navy wife but who cares. You're mine."

"Good, now we can talk about what I want to talk about."

"And that is?"

"Now that I am 25, I am very rich."

"I thought you were rich before, that's why I married you."

"No, before I had money but today, I get my mother's money along with what my father put aside. He did not trust me and still doesn't but now the money is mine."

"Good for you but how does that concern us?"

"I want to spend the money."

"Go ahead. Spend it anyway you like."

"You don't care?"

"No. Just make sure there is enough for Alexandra and our old age."

"You will help me?"

"Yes but only when this war is over. Right now, I have a job to do."

"When the war is over, we will have much fun."

"I thought we already are having fun?"

"Nestor, I will make you so happy after the war."

After their breakfast in bed, Christiana and Eric explored Manhattan taking a double-decker bus down Fifth Avenue. They retraced their bus route on foot, walking past store windows, kissing in doorways. A cab brought them to Central Park, where they rode a white horse-drawn carriage as dusk settled on the city.

Behind the plodding horse, she rested in his arms.

"Nestor, I must tell you something else."

"What is it?"

"My Duenas is very sick."

"I did not know that."

"Yes, she wants to go home to her village to die."

"Shouldn't we first see if we can save her?"

"I have had to all the best doctors in Washington. There is no hope."

"I am sorry Christiana. I know what she means to you. And to Alexandra."

"Yes it will be hard on her as well."

"So what do you need from me?"

"She will not survive a boat trip or going by train. Too long and arduous."

"There are planes. You want me to arrange it."

"Yes and for me too."

"Why you."

"Because she has been with me since I was born. Now she needs me."

"I can get you there but it will be tough getting you back."

Laughing, Christiana tightened her hold on his body. "I will come back to you, I promise. Just get us there."

They laughed together, hoping to dispel the sadness they felt. After a few minutes, Eric pushed away and looked her in the face.

"You know what today is?"

"Of course, it is my 25th birthday and you haven't wished me happy birthday enough. Nor any gift but this buggy ride."

"I was waiting for the right moment."

"Now? You want to undress me now, here?"

"No, that will come later. Now is the time I give you this. It is the only legacy my family has."

Eric gave her his mother's emerald necklace, cherished in his family for three generations. She knew about the jewel but never thought of it as hers, expecting it would go to Alexandra. Placing it around her neck, he kissed her.

"You are mine forever," he said to her as they hugged in the twilight of the May Day.

After making love that night, Eric left in the early morning for his Boston train. Not wanting to overnight away from her, he took the last train back to New York that Monday.

Running for the train, Eric snagged flowers from the station vendor, throwing money at the man in passing. Impatient to see her, he rapidly paced the few blocks to the Waldorf Astoria, almost skipping in his joy. The attendant chuckled as the officer brushed by him.

When Christiana did not answer his knocks, he impatiently called the man to open the door. Christiana lay across the bed, naked, bloody, with eyes wide in shock.

Forever had lasted a day.

# May, 1943
## Giovanni Perrone

With many of its younger officers drafted or volunteered into the armed forces, World War II shook up the New York City police force. Besides putting older officers back on the streets, various detective bureaus saw an influx of younger crime experts. None rose higher or quicker than Lieutenant Giovanni Perrone. Envied by some, he led the Manhattan murder squad at 34. When asked why he was not in the army, he pointed to his feet, which, early in the war, kept many men from enlisting. As manpower needs grew, this .deferment was waived.

What got him his promotions was his obsessive observation of details. This attention to things his fellow officers ignored enabled him to rise rapidly from patrolman to detective and then command, faster than anyone in the department could remember.

Getting off the elevator on The President's floor before the sun rose on that Tuesday morning, he noted the doors still shut in the other rooms. Their occupants were too concerned with their affairs not peeking out as would be the case in hotels and apartment buildings less pocketed with VIPs than the Waldorf Astoria. He saw the manager hovering around his sergeant, who wore an exasperated look as he directed photographers and other technicians. Seeing higher authority approaching, he gave the man touching his arm, a nod indicating Perrone was the man to speak to.

"Your people won't let my guests leave this floor," the thin acerbic man pleaded at Perrone.

"Not till we get statements and verify who they are."

"You can take my word for them."

"Not good enough."

"But you don't understand."

Oh, I do. Some people in these rooms shouldn't be there."

Visibly relieved, the man in charge understood his worry; he relaxed somewhat.

"Then I can rely on your discretion."

"We're looking for a crazy murderer. Not hanky panky." Perrone assured the man, not telling him about the call from his boss urging discretion.

"How could it happen in my hotel?"

"That's what we want to find out. Especially as you have a night porter there to screen every visitor."

"Paul is one of my most reliable people."

"Maybe he slipped and fell asleep. Or, he let somebody in he shouldn't have let in. Let's talk with him now."

"He's pretty shook up."

"Good, then maybe he'll make a slip or remember something."

Paul's real name was Reginald Watkins, but when he first applied for a job at the Waldorf 21 years before, the hiring clerk couldn't bother remembering the name of the scared kid before him, so he was entered into the logbook as Paul Warren. The name stuck until social security was introduced and Reginald Watkins was on his birth certificate. At the Waldorf Astoria, he was Paul Reginald Watkins, known to everyone as just plain Paul.

Sitting slumped by himself alone, even in the crowded corridor, Perrone touched the man's shoulder.

"I've seen the woman on the bed. It was awful. She was so alive so nice so kind. Don't want to see nothin' like that agin'. She must've suffered and that ain't good."

"When did you last see her?"

"About 7:30. She came in with some packages and asked for some drinks. I think Manhattans. It'll be on the slips. Henry brought them from the bar on the floor below. Musta been about 8 o'clock".

"Did you go into the room?"

"He did. Just for a moment. She signed and went to answer the phone."

"The phone rang."

"Henry closed the door for her as she answered the phone."

"Did Henry hear anything?"

"You gotta ask him. He's back at three."

"Anyway someone can get on this floor past you?"

"Only the backstairs we use and they would need a key."

"Are all the keys accounted for?"

"We're not sure. Sometimes the maids bring them home by mistake. I'll check."

The detective gave him a moment to collect his thoughts. Then said.

"So, someone can come on the floor through the backstairs. Yes, if they have a key or someone is waiting to open the door. They use the elevator to go two floors down and then walk up two flights. Sometimes some of guests prefer we not log them in. If they show up without a guest, we're supposed to ask for a name?"

"Do they usually give it to you?"

"You'd be surprised at how many Mary Joneses and Martha Washingtons there are in this world."

"Ever been paid to not write a name?"

"Don't need that trouble. This a great job and I've been here 21 years don't need that trouble."

"Did the victim have any of these visitors?"

"Not a one but a girlfriend came up Friday. She was sure into her husband. Acted more like lovers than husband and wives."

"Are you sure he came in after 1am?"

"He smelled as if he just came off a train. We get that a lot here what with Grand Central so close. They usually head for the shower first after ordering drinks. He didn't even ask for a drink when he got off the elevator."

"You didn't hear anything from the room before he came in?"

"We're usually quiet on Monday nights. Just had five rooms occupied. Two are regular gentlemen in from Chicago. Don't know what they do but here every month. There's Mrs. Barkly, she's on her way to Long Branch to their summer home. But the Coast Guard or someone are holding them up. There's Sam Katz, he produces movies and here for an opening. Stays here when he's expecting his wife elsewhere when she's not coming, if you know what I mean. And then there's this Professor from Princeton who is giving a lecture someplace in town. For some reason the FBI check us out before allowing him to stay here. Came in and went to his room and as far as I know is still there."

"You seem to know your clients pretty well?"

"Knowing them and what they need means a bigger tip when they leave."

"What about the victim?"

"Well I'll tell you. Never met one like her. Beautiful. Nice. Kind. Good tipper. And she sure adored that officer. You see married couples come in and not look at each other the whole time. I thought they were lovers but she showed me pictures of her daughter. Surprised the hell out of me."

"In what way?"

"That they were married that long and she was so young. Do you know yesterday...no Sunday was her 25th birthday? He gave her some emerald she said was his mother's. Seem to mean a lot to her. I wonder who's going to tell that child her mother's gone?"

"I wonder that as well."

Steeling himself, Perrone left the porter and entered the murder room. Stabbing deaths are always messy. Stains were scattered on walls, floors, and bedcoverings. Christiana was nude, her slip torn with two pieces in her mouth.

She fought valiantly from the bruises on her arms and shoulders to avoid rape and, finally, her execution. The medical examiner representative was finishing his work and motioned for the two ambulance men to stop ogling the body and transport it to the morgue.

Perrone examined the room more closely. The drink vase and two glasses were on the desk, and the flowers he assumed the husband had brought lay trampled on the floor. Her dress from the previous day was hung on the door. Her bathrobe, which he believed she donned to get the drinks lay torn on the bed. The bolt chain was intact but dangled from its hook unused.

Seeing the man was an assistant to the medical examiner Perrone knew he needed to wait for more formal evidence until the complete autopsy. But he asked one question: Time of death.

"I'm guessing but no later than 11pm and probably closer to 9pm," the man said.

"Will that time hold up after the autopsy?

"I'm pretty certain. Temperature, lividity both point that way."

"Husband says he was in Boston till catching a 9pm train?"

"Those flowers are from a Boston florist and still fresh."

"Guess we can eliminate him quickly."

The body and technician left Perrone and two crime lab staff behind. To the hotel manager's relief, they left the hotel discreetly by a side door unobserved by other guests in the lobby.

After asking his team to take statements from the other guests and directed by his sergeant, Perrone went into the empty room down the hall from the murder scene to talk with the shaken husband.

"Sorry to bother you at a time like this." Perrone began.

"Ask away. I need to do something to keep my mind off of what I saw in there."

"It must have been tough."

"Yesterday we talked about forever and today it ended. Why? Everyone loved Christiana. Who could do such a thing?"

"That's what we want to find out."

"To attend a wedding and have a vacation."

Who got married."

"Big Tony Massucci's daughter."

"No kidding and you got invited."

"Yes, I liaison with him for the Navy."

"Why liaison with that scum?"

"Because he can make things happen on the docks. Or not happen. I worry about getting supplies to our boys. There's time enough after this war to deal with his other activities."

"Sensible approach. Don't usually hear this from Navy or Army people."

"Sometimes the people on top think with their heads and not their asses."

"Anything happen at the wedding?"

"No, nothing unusual for Christiana. Wherever she went she met people and made friends. She was magnet. Sometimes men would misinterpret her but she usually kept them friendly."

"Make you jealous?"

"No," he laughed. "She chose me at a party in Caracas and I have never had to doubt her. We just celebrated her 25th birthday yesterday...er Sunday. Funny, this weekend was the first vacation we've had since our honeymoon. She was pregnant when we got married and spent the honeymoon and next three months in the bathroom."

"So no one gave her trouble at the wedding or afterward?"

"No."

"Who knew you were in town?"

"No one and everyone. I toured the docks Friday and went to Boston yesterday for a meeting. But I wasn't expected to see anyone in particular."

"I had a report she got a phone call about 8pm. That you?"

"No, I was rushing to catch a train. I wanted to be here. We needed to go back to Washington later today."

"She would answer the phone even though you weren't here."

"She has friends all over. Friday, she met one and they went all over the city."

"Yeah, I heard about her. So, you know of no one who would want to call you or her."

"No, if my Admiral wanted me, he could get me at the meeting in Boston. We were scheduled to meet later today. Anything else would have waited."

"Well we usually look hard at the husband in a case like this but our medical examiner thinks she was killed while you were in Boston. So, if you want to go back to Washington to talk to your daughter you can."

"I don't know what to do. I want to wait till I can bring her home but don't want Alexandra to hear about her mother from some reporter or well-meaning friend."

"Tell you what, go home, and I'll try to expedite things so you can bring her home on Thursday."

"That would be a kindness."

"Least I can do."

Turning over what Eric told him, Perrone gathered his team, and they reviewed notes. Nothing came out of their exchanges except verification that one key to the side door was missing. Perrone detailed one man to interview the day staff as they came on duty.

He reserved for himself the task of talking to the hotel operators. Knowing the night crew didn't start until 4pm, he spent part of the day questioning bellhops and the front desk, asking if any loiterers were noticed.

Putting the arm on the manager, he was given a free lunch in one of the hotel restaurants after spending time looking at guest slips for the President's floor in the back office. This exercise told him nothing except he couldn't afford to stay at the Waldorf Astoria.

Perrone thought his day was wasted from answers from the first two nighttime operators who came on. Two other operators reported no calls, but he got his first lead when the last shift worker came on.

"You know it's funny. My first call last night was for their room," Gladys Harwin said.

"Why do you remember it?"

"Because it was muffled and came from the house phone downstairs."

"Is that unusual?"

"Go see it. You've really got to know this hotel to even find it."

"It's used by certain ladies to announce themselves when they arrive via the side entrance. That way they don't parade through the main lobby."

"What do you mean muffled."

"Like he didn't want anyone to hear him even me."

"Did they ask for him or her."

"Oh, for the officer. Said he didn't know the rank and didn't know the room. Just the name."

"First he said Dickman, than he paused and then said Dykman as if he was reading from a card."

"I checked and rang through but no one answered."

"Did he have the room number?"

"Not this time but when he called back an hour later he just said the room number."

"Did anyone answer?"

"No, again no answer and he hung up."

"Why do you know it was the same person?"

"I'm here 12 years and I know my job. If he was a suspicious person, I call security to check 'em out."

"Were the calls from the same phone."

"Yes, that's why I'm remembering it so well."

"Did he call back again?"

"Yes, he did about 8pm before my break. This time she answered. I heard her voice before cutting out of the conversation."

"Did it sound as if she knew him?"

"No, he called her Mrs. Dykman."

"Thank you Gladys, you've been a great help."

"Should I have called security?"

"Yes, I am afraid you should have."

Together with what Gladys said, Perrone walked downstairs into the shopping corner below the hotel's main lobby. He found the hidden call phone down the lower hall, and Perrone needed to know how the individual knew about it. The investigator walked to the side entrance and saw several bars and coffee shops across the street. Before he tackled them, he turned to the stores along the corridor. Only one looked occupied at the moment, a florist. He went in, not expecting much but hopeful.

"Hear about the murder upstairs."

"All anyone can talk about. I'm waiting for the News to come. Hear they got pictures."

"You here yesterday?"

"Every day but Sunday. It's my shop with my dad."

"See any suspicious characters hanging around?"

"If they hang around, I call the hotel dicks,"

"Do that yesterday?"

"Didn't need to. There was a passel of foreign cops and some locals milling around all day. Someone important must be in the building."

"See anyone come in and go to the phone over there."

"I try not to notice. The hotel has it there for a reason. So, no one will notice who uses it."

"But if someone used it more than once you'd notice."

"Yeah, it's funny. Just as I was leaving around 7pm a guy came to use it. It's usually a dame or a young stud but he was older. And from the looks of him someone you didn't want to talk to."

"Did he use the phone."

"I think he rang a room but no one answered. He hung up and walked out."

"Did you see him again."

"Could have. I went home. My dad closed up about nine. Ask him he'll be back in a few minutes. He's smoking a cigar. Can't smoke in the shop otherwise the tobacco smell gets on the flowers."

When the older proprietor arrived, he said the man was back about 8pm, and this time the party answered, and he went upstairs. He hadn't returned by the time he closed his shop.

Pleased with himself, Perrone went door to door asking about a man who loitered for two hours the night before. He was rewarded with two similar descriptions of the same man from a coffee shop and bar.

Armed with this information, he went home to think about his next step. Instead of going to his squad room, Perrone went downtown to FBI headquarters to talk to his only friend amongst the feds. This friend referred him to the Special Agent-in-Charge.

"I bet you have pictures of everyone at Big Tony Massucci's wedding on Saturday," Perrone open the conversation.

"So does your department's gang unit."

"Yeah, and you know and I know the minute I ask for them Big Tony will know."

"You think he did your murder. With his dick he doesn't need to rape some South American heiress."

"Is that who she was."

"Yeah with a naval officer for a husband and some people in Washington upset. Say he's needed for the war effort."

"Think he did it."

"No, he was in Boston. I have a good description of who did do it but need some pictures to get some witnesses to ID."

"Why should we give you a set."

"Use to be we were on the same side."

"Still are," the agent said, reaching into his desk and giving Perrone a thick set of prints.

"Thanks, did not hope to get such cooperation."

"I got a call from Washington. Said to help as much as possible. Apparently, this Naval Officer is scheduled to go overseas in two weeks. Tough break."

"Tougher if I can't identify the guy."

When he arrived in his squad room, the room was abuzz.

"We got another death," his Sergeant greeted him.

"And that concerns us."

"The one maid we haven't spoken with. Pushed under a subway last night."

"Did she have access to keys."

"Yep and the missing key was on her."

"Fingerprints?"

"Funny you asked, wiped clean."

"Her name?"

"Angela Parisi."

"Related to anyone in Big Tony's gang?"

"Yeah, Augie Parisi, her brother.
But he couldn't have done it. He's in Sing Sing."

"Another dead end."

"So let's show our witnesses some pictures."

Returning to the Waldorf Astoria, Perrone and his Sergeant asked father and son to pick out anyone they saw. Both men recoiled when they realized the photos were from Big Tony's wedding event.

Like many citizens, they both immediately feared getting involved. Sensing their fear, Perrone watched their faces. When they came to the picture of Sal Vassallo, both men looked at the other. They passed over the man, but Perrone now knew who had used the cellar phone.

Learning how not to show the FBI photos, Perrone went back to headquarters and sought pictures of other gangsters along with Vassallo's. Armed with a photo array, he sought out the witnesses from the previous night.

They identified Vassallo but could only place him outside the hotel. His mistake cost him any chance of getting the two florists to identify the murderer.

Stymied, he did the only thing open to him; Perrone released Christiana's body and traveled with it to Washington. The next step would be up to Eric.

# May, 1943
## Eric Dykman

From the time America integrated its railroads, officials required individuals to accompany bodies being moved by rail. Their preference was to have some official from the originating jurisdiction be chosen for the task.

In time members of the deceased's family were permitted to accompany the coffin on the rails in place of an official. With this requirement came eerie tales told by solitary travelers uneasy with their task.

Among railroad workers, there grew lore about the strange happenings in the dark cars during the dead of night. Alone, standing guard next to the coffin, many civilians who performed the task reported weird incidents such as bodies rising from the coffins, noises as if the dead were talking, or even apparitions leaving the bier. Many could not be explained.

When the time came for Christiana Dykman's body to be transported from New York to Washington, Police Lt. Giovanni Perrone did not want her to make this last journey alone with a stranger.

Against precedents, he chose to make the journey. To allay the widower's questions, he said it would be an honor to accompany the body as he was coming for the funeral anyway.

As he told her husband by phone, often in murder cases, coming to the funeral was part of the investigation to see if any suspicious mourner appeared. Rightly guessing the daughter was not taking events well, he told Eric to stay with his daughter and family.

Perrone also did something else out of character for the jaded detective concerned about how they treated the victim's body. Knowing how the medical examiner dissected and mutilated other murder victims, he arranged for the body to be reassembled as much as possible.

Even with his intervention, it was still necessary to tell the family the funeral would be a closed coffin ceremony. This badly shocked Eric and his father-in-law. Neither quite comprehended how badly Christiana was treated at the hands of her murderer. Eric's brief glimpse of his wife's body did not fully show how badly her assailant cut through her body.

Since the first meeting, a tight bond developed between the two men. Never had Perrone ever experienced such feelings towards the victim's family. He couldn't explain why this man or the victim affected him, but the feeling was so strong he drove his squad with 24-hour tours.

Four days had passed since the body was discovered, and Perrone's gut strongly implied he had the murderer in his sight. The tricky part came, proving Sal Vassallo raped and murdered Christiana Dykman.

Alone with her body in the railway mail car going between New York and Washington, Perrone weighed his options. If he told Eric Dykman of his suspicions, he risked the grieving widower doing something rash like confronting Vassallo. In such a meeting, the gangster would have no qualms about killing the Naval Officer.

After three fruitless conversations with the florists, he knew they would never testify against the perpetrator. The key letting him onto the hotel floor almost certainly came from Angela Parisi, and she was dead now too. Another loose end tied up by the madman.

Looking at his police file, Perrone was convinced now Vassallo was a madman. Shuddering at the thought, even if he could charge Vassallo, Perrone also believed the criminal could escape justice by claiming insanity.

Sitting alone in the car's rear, he heard the postal workers in the forward end sorting mail. They only needed to deliver the mail; he was tasked with providing sad news. He didn't think that was the role he relished.

Tipped off by an informal grapevine, family and friends packed the train platform when Christiana's coffin arrived. Opening the side doors, two porters hopped into the postal car and gently lifted her coffin onto a waiting cart. Perrone followed at a distance, pushed aside by the crush of people expressing their anguish.

Placed on the rolling cart, the coffin proceeded the crowd through the back corridors to where a hearse was waiting. Before entering the car behind the hearse, Perrone managed to push his way to Eric's side. Exchanging wordless glances, the men got into Christiana's yellow Buick along with an older gentleman and followed the coffin onto the District of Columbia streets.

"Enrique, this is the police officer in charge of Christiana's case," Eric said without looking back from following the hearse.

"Do you know who did this to my daughter?" Enrique del la Vega shouted at the policeman.

"We're getting a pretty good picture."

"So you know," Eric said.

"Not with a certainty I can say to you."

"But you think you know?"

"We've got some good leads."

"Was it someone at the wedding?"

"You know I can't say too much."

"But you know, don't you? Enrique shouted at the man.

Looking away, Perrone said with some finality: "Knowing and proving are two very different things."

"What can I do to help you?" Eric said.

"You can bury your wife and let me do my job."

"Then why are you here? Why aren't you back in New York finding the evidence you need?" Eric said with some bitterness.

"Because one thing we always do is go to the victim's funeral. Sometimes, the murderer shows up to gloat or satisfy some curiosity. That's why I'm here. And also, because I want to be here. I don't know why but she and you are important to me."

"Better if you'd stayed in New York. We're having the funeral on Monday. Nobody will come it's a work day."

"I just want to see who comes."

"Where are you staying?"

"I'll find a hotel."

"No, we have room, stay with us," Enrique quickly piped up.

"Yes, stay with us," Eric echoed.

Hearing the hurt in his voice, Perrone quickly agreed.

# May, 1943
## Enrique de la Vega

Houses take on the aura of their occupants. Where families reside in reasonable harmony, their homes seem somehow cheerier. Buildings serving transients never seem part of the neighborhood, but rather interlopers placed there temporarily. Homes enable occupants to put down roots, but houses remain subject to changing occupants.

When Lt. Giovanni Perrone entered the home Christiana de la Vega bought, he sensed a house of pain. Sitting silently in the corner on the first floor was a dark-skinned older woman, neither Latino nor Indian. Holding a wrapped doll, she was staring off into space, oblivious to the noise and talk around her. Taken to his second-floor room, he saw another woman holding her teacup close to her breast and walking up the stairs to the third floor.

Placing his small suitcase on the bed, he wandered down the hall to the kitchen, where a cook, maid, and the man who had chauffeured them from the station silently sat at the table. Not wanting to disturb them, he walked downstairs to the main floor finding Eric and Enrique engaged in earnest conversation. They stopped when they saw him.

"We were going through the funeral arrangements," Eric explained.

"My daughter was not religious, but I want her buried from a church."

"The problem is what church," Eric said.

"It seems my daughter has two priests fighting to have her in their church."

"That's a problem?" Perrone asked.

"It seems my daughter made great friends with both and they are arguing outside."

"Which is the most convenient?" Perrone asked innocently.

"You don't understand. One priest is pastor of the Cathedral and the other is the Archbishop. How my daughter knows both and being,

138

how you say, disinclined to religion they are insisting. Even dispensing with the need to prove she was in, how do you say, without sin."

"My wife continues to amaze me lieutenant," Eric said and began almost crying.

"I'd take the cathedral. Give her a great send off," Perrone said without thinking.

"I agree," Enrique said.

"So be it. I don't know how Alexandra is going to take all this."

" Kids are stronger than we think."

"Deborah will help her get through this," Enrique said with finality.

"You know I need to leave for England very soon," Eric said to both men.

"Deborah and I will take care of Alexandra," Enrique said.

"What are we going to do with the Duena?" Eric asked.

"One of my sons is coming up. He will be anxious to go back to Caracas as soon as possible. He will take her."

"Are you sure. They don't seem to me to be the caring type."

"I assure you, this they will do."

"Well the only thing left is make sure Alexandra is okay." Eric said.

"Deborah will see to that," Enrique said in such a way as to reassure the father and policeman.

The solemnity of the evening was broken by Alexandra's laughter as she sat next to Deborah de Courcy. Christiana's two sisters-in-law and their children, Enrique, Eric, and Perrone. Even with the laughter, he felt the sadness in everyone's hearts.

He noticed how Enrique's eyes always strayed to the child and her playmate throughout the meal. It took him through the desert to finally surmise that the older man was not looking at Alexandra but Deborah. "You old dog, you, Perrone said to himself. There must be 25 years between them. Deborah was a striking difference in this household with her English accent, light hair, and robust figure.

Even with his background as a police officer, Perrone was put off by the old woman in the corner. So far as he could tell, she had not moved since he entered the house. Everyone else also seemed to ignore her, and when he went to bed and rose in the morning, she was there.

The weekend passed uneventfully as preparations were made for the funeral and reception afterward. Deciding to dispense with a weekend wake and determining only Eric and Enrique, they left the rest of the mass to the Archbishop's discretion. Alexandra also said she wanted to add her voice, and neither her father nor grandfather could say no.

On Monday, when the family arrived at the Cathedral, the crowd of mourners almost filled the main chapel. This did not surprise Deborah, Marvel, or the sisters-in-law. Even in Washington, Christiana's ability to attract and win friends from all walks of life was clearly evident to them.

For Perrone, the large crowd, his hope of finding a possible suspect grew near impossible. There were ordinary individuals such as cab drivers, druggists, three policemen, and the man who washed her yellow Buick. Two senators came, a cabinet officer, and five South American Ambassadors. The Venezuelan ambassador and Christiana's childhood friend from New York were in the front row. A somber crowd came for the woman who did not know how to be sad.

One of the Senators gravely walked up to Marvel Huntington as she stood next to Alexandra.

"Perhaps you don't remember me," he said, expecting a positive reply given his office.

"Oh, do I ever senator, you were coming out of that hotel with the woman not your wife when you spotted your wife."

"Yes, that was a difficult moment and Mrs. Dykman certainly helped me," he said embarrassingly.

"She sure did, taking your arm and brazenly walking up to your wife, explaining our meeting as one for war bonds. What was your wife going to say then?"

"Certainly, helped me out. She had heard some rumor about me and a young lady."

"More than a rumor if what I saw that day."

"A momentary indiscretion I assure you."

Isn't me needing reassurance. Glad it all worked out."

"It did and has. Please convey to Captain Dykman my condolences and gratitude for knowing his wife. Should he ever need a favor, have him call me."

"That I will Senator as long as that invitation includes my husband, Captain Huntington as well."

"I assure you it does."

"Then maybe some good may come out of this tragedy."

"Let us hope so for that young child's sake." And with that, he wandered off.

As the reception ended, one elderly man dignified in his chauffer's uniform shouldered his way through to Eric. He handed him embossed stationery and retreated into the crowd without saying anything. Opening the envelope, he saw it was from Alice Roosevelt Longworth. Washington doyenne, surprised by its warm condolences, Eric turned to Marvel.

"Christiana had heard so much about the woman when we passed her house, she told the driver to stop," Marvel replied to his questioning look.

"And she naturally walked in?" he said, half-amused at this tragic time.

"Well, you knew Christiana; breezing in, she met the woman, and the two got into a conversation quite ignoring me. From that day onward, Alice used Christiana to get things done. Christiana got invited to all the top events, thanks to Alice. I went along on a lot of them. You never realized how popular she was until today."

"That's for sure. Did I ever really know my wife?

"All you need to know was she loved you. She'd drop everything the minute she knew you were home."

"That's good enough for me."

"No man would want more."

Washington newspapers reported about the reception afterward, calling it one of the most democratic in memory, given the mix of people who came to say goodbye. The star of the day was Alexandra, who carried off the role of a stoic bereaved daughter with great dignity.

With Deborah and Eric, she broke down and cried herself to sleep in her room, and the woman stayed with her that night. Within a week, she had become friend, nanny, teacher, and family. These roles became doubly important when Eric finally told her of his impending separation. Alexandra cried for almost 24-hours clinging to Deborah.

Heartbroken at his assignment, Eric tried to get his orders changed but was told other soldiers and sailors made similar sacrifices, and he was needed in Europe.

After the funeral reception, Perrone went back to New York to try to get more evidence against Vassallo. All his efforts failed, and he was left with nothing else to do but tell Eric of his failure. This he would do when the Naval Officer came through the city on his way to England.

Their meeting led to one of the most defining moments in his life. A moment he came to regret.

# June, 1943
## Anthony "Big Tony" Massucci

In the criminal underworld, leaders earned their positions through violence. Because the extent of their menace marked their rise, they ruled by fear. In Twentieth-Century American gangsterism, there was no more effective way to maintain fear among mob disciples than by periodic acts of murder. Anthony "Big Tony" Massucci knew this better than anyone. According to the New York Police Department, he practiced this approach more than any other union boss in their area.

The tool for carrying out these periodic purges was Sal Vassallo. No one knew what hold Big Tony had over the man most thought was insane, but the union boss kept Sal in tow. But when loosed, Sal had a brutal way of dispatching victims. It involved garroting them with a silk tie and lifting the target off his feet. The effect was to slowly strangle the man. Once dead, Sal left another tie around the neck, keeping the actual murder weapon as a souvenir.

It was never reported that someone had seen the inside of Sal's room in a Red Hook Brooklyn boardinghouse. Rumors abounded that he kept his ties from each murder in his closet. No one wanted to verify the tale.

In the days after Christiana Dykman's death, police Lt. Giovanni Perrone spent his time shadowing Sal and attempting to link him to her gruesome death. When Sal finally identified his shadow, he laughed in Perrone's face. Sure, there was nothing more he could do; Perrone shelved the case, angry at himself and the law.

# June, 1943
## Eric Dykman

Eric parted with his daughter, knowing she was even more broken-hearted. His deployment, coupled with the sting of his wife's death, put him in fear the child would be forever haunted. His orders put him on a train to New York to pick up his ride to England.

During World War II, new B-17 bombers being flown to England as replacements in many cases were shuttled across the Atlantic by women pilots. Lightened to enable them to fly almost non-stop, certain flights accommodated high-priority individuals or equipment. One such flight procurement was made for Eric Dykman. When he arrived in the city, he was annoyed to learn there was a 24-hour delay due to weather, leaving him alone in the city with such an unpleasant memory.

Reluctantly but hoping to hear more about the case, he went to the precinct where Perrone's squad room was situated to take up his waiting time. Held at the front lobby while calls were made to the detectives, Perrone hastily came down to talk with the man whose wife's loss still rankled.

Taken to a side room, the men sat across the table. Eric in his naval uniform and Perrone as always neatly attired.

"You can't tell me anymore?" Eric asked.

"It's still ongoing."

"But you have a good idea?"

"I can't say."

"We're alone in this room. I'm headed to England."

"I can't prove it."

"So, what can you tell me?"

"Nothing really."

"Please Giovanni,"

"What could you do if I did."

"I don't know. I certainly wouldn't go out and get a gun to kill him."

"Even if you had a gun, you couldn't use it and he would kill you."

"So, you know, you know, you know."

"Let's put it this way, I have enough to know if I could sweat it out of him, I would. But this guy is a special case, and he's nuts."

"Nuts? Like you mean certifiable?"

"Yes, even if I got him to court, he would get off because even his associates know he's nuts."

"So, you're saying he's a mob guy."

"I'm not saying anything."

"But it was someone at that wedding we went to the weekend before she died."

"Eric, I can't say anything more."

"But maybe I can talk to someone who can say more."

"Who do you mean?"

"Big Tony."

Don't mess with him."

"What do I lose? I'm in England the day after tomorrow."

"If he lets you get on the plane."

"He will because you're coming with me and bringing the file."

"Are you crazy?"

"No, just enough to convince him. I'll do the rest."

Angry, he couldn't do more; Giovanni sat there for a few minutes and went to get his coat and some papers. It took the men several hours to find Big Tony. Sitting in the back of his Mulberry Street social club, he narrowed his eyes when he saw it was Eric standing there with the police lieutenant.

"Good to see you, Captain. Sorry about your wife," Big Tony said cautiously.

"Good to see you, but I'm here to find the man who murdered her.

"And for that, you brought the cops."

"Wanted him to show you his findings,"

"Why me?"

"Because one of your men did it."

"Which one? The mob boss sat up straight and stiffened.

"He won't tell me, but I was hoping he can either tell you or get pointed in the right direction."

"What makes you think one of my people did it."

"I'm going to keep quiet and let him talk."

For the next 15 minutes, Giovanni outlined his case to Big Tony, who sat and listened. At the end of the recital, Big Tony looked at the policeman and in a flat voice said: "Nobody you describe comes to mind. You're wrong because I asked all of the people at the wedding when I heard. Go peddle your crap somewhere else."

With that, he dismissed the two men, who left.

"Well, that didn't go over too well," Eric said.

"Don't feel too bad. It was one of his men and I think he'll dispense his own sentence.

"You think so."

"He's a mobster, not a monster. What's more, he's leading an organization where all these guys got wives and mistresses. They're going to wonder if this guy is going to take a fancy to one of them. They're criminals, not sex fiends. Having a sex fiend in their midst is dangerous. What happened to your wife can't be condoned. What happened to your wife was more than they can allow to continue. I would go back to your hotel and wait. He's not going to call me, but I think he will call you. They have their own way of working, and that does not include calling the cops."

There was silence in the mob clubhouse as the two men left. Since he first heard about Christiana's death, he harbored suspicions. He never confronted Sal directly, but Big Tony remembered the man was not around in the days following the wedding.

With what the cop just showed him, Big Tony knew it was Sal in the lobby of the Waldorf Astoria. He also knew the man had no mob business there. Sal had done many things for Big Tony. Many of which should not see the light of day.

He also knew how dangerous Sal would be if cornered. The need now was to act fast before someone inadvertently tipped off the killer. Big Tony knew if Sal felt threatened, he would lash out in his direction.

Calling together his four most trusted subordinates, he saw two faces blanched when told of the need to stop Sal. All four knew of the strength and viciousness inherent in the man.

Leaving word at Sal's boardinghouse to join him at a mob warehouse, Big Tony prepared carefully for the killer's arrival. A cargo net was rigged to fall on him when entering the building. The four men stood by with lethal saps should he somehow struggle free. Straps and chains were also set up with two pistols and a shotgun. All were expected to be used against the man they all feared.

Getting the message, Sal took a cab to the warehouse, confident his fearsome reputation made him invincible. Strolling into the building, the heavy net stung him, and four men piled on top of him. None of the other men worried about hurting each other in their fear-driven desire to subdue their quarry.

Despite his great strength, even Sal could not prevail against his tormentors, and soon he was trussed tightly with netting, rope, and chains. Panting heavily, the four men brought him in front of Big Tony,

"The naval officer and a cop met with me today, Sal," said the mob boss.

"Did they each blow you?" Sal sneered.

"No. Showed me some pictures and witness statements."

"A cop showed you his file?"

"Yeah, he did. Funny people picked you out from an array."

"From where?"

"The Waldorf Astoria where the Navy officer's wife was killed."

"Don't know anything about that."

"Sure you do. She and you were at my daughter's wedding."

"I didn't go."

"Yes, you did. I saw you there."

"So maybe I was but not at the Waldorf. Too uptown for me."

"What about Angela Parisi?"

"Augie says you knew her."

"Know a lot of women, just like you."

"Yeah, but most of them go out with you once and then are scared to death of you."

"It's my charm."

"Sal, you've done a lot for me."

"Don't you know it?"

"But this is too far."

"What's this?"

"From the pictures, I saw you beat that woman before knifing her."

"She wouldn't cooperate."

"So you admit it?"

"Why not. What are you going to do?"

"Me, nothing, but I'm making a phone call."

"To the cops?"

"No, her husband."

"Let him come. I'll break him in two."

Big Tony went into the warehouse office and sent two men to fetch the Navy Captain. Eric was surprised when one showed up at his hotel door, inviting him for a ride. Without calling Giovanni, he followed the man to their waiting car. When they arrived at the warehouse, Eric walked into a dimly lit cavernous space with Sal at the center.

"Your cop pal asked me if I knew who killed your wife," Big Tony said.

"Yes, he did."

"At the time, I didn't. Sal here just told me he did it."

Eric looked at the bound man and shivered. Sal spewed hatred from his face and tried to struggle to his feet, and the men behind him clobbered him with a blackjack. He fell back hurt but not subdued.

"I can't bring your wife back, but I can give you the means to revenge her," Big Tony said quietly.

"What do you mean?"

"Here's an untraceable gun. Shoot him. It will give you some measure of relief."

Looking at the gun, Eric shuddered again at the bound man. For two minutes, Sal's life hung in the balance. Eric was having trouble speaking, even thinking. His hatred of the man filled him with anger. Then what happened haunted him for the rest of his life.

"You want me to kill this man in cold blood?"

"For what he did to your wife."

"I can't."

"Not even for your wife's honor."

"I don't think she would want this honor."

"Then I can let him go?"

"If you must, yes. I can't kill this man."

"I don't know whether you're a fool or a great man."

"Neither, just someone who knows he can't kill. Even for the most extraordinary woman he will ever know.

"So be it. Take him back to his hotel. You're leaving for England tomorrow. Be sure you're on that plane."

When Eric left, Big Tony turned to Sal.

"Who would've thought I'd be saved by a pantywaist Navy boy."

"What makes you think he saved you."

"You ain't going to kill me over some Latino broad."

"No, Sal, not for killing the woman. But because no one in our organization will feel safe with you around...and that includes me."

"I won't kill you Big Tony we go back too far."

"Yes, we do Sal. But you also put a lot of dock guys' jobs in jeopardy. If that Captain had wanted to, he could have scuttled our little arrangement. We had it nice here on the docks and you almost fucked it up. No, I have permission to kill you. How I do it is up to me. I would have preferred for the captain to do it but he chickened out. Now it is up to me. You're a dead man Sal. May God rest your soul."

# May, 1943
## Eric Dykman

Sorrow is an emotion even distances do not assuage. Eric thought putting an ocean between him and the tragic events in New York would help ease the pain of his loss. Leaving his daughter, Alexandra, with her grandfather and Deborah DeCourcy was not easy. With the fierce war raging worldwide, he consoled himself by realizing other men and women were also leaving loved ones behind.

Recognizing the terrible events could not be erased, he spent his last night in the city alone, half-drunk and pining for the woman he lost. Realizing he had also failed at revenge made his loss even more difficult to bear. With little religious faith to ease his mind, he had no one or faith to alleviate his pain.

The thoughts whirling through his mind gave him no solace during the cab ride to Floyd Bennett Field in Queens. They all seemed to foretell a lifetime of regrets. Dimmed or shut street lamps added darker shadows in the pre-dawn darkness of the deserted streets. After a year of torpedoed ships just off the coast, the city had learned to shut off any illumination that helped enemy U-boats.

Situated hard by the coast, Floyd Bennett Field served the war effort as an anti-submarine base and gateway to planes flying the North Atlantic route to Europe. In Eric's case, the need for replacing parts in two engines forced the newly minted B-17 to detour to New York to get them installed.

Hardly reassuring, he was surprised to learn it was being flown to England by two women pilots. Shrugging away any thoughts he had on the subject, take-off was scheduled for 7am. It was 5am when Eric's cab pulled up to the gate. Swiftly confirmed, he took his bag and walked to the ready lounge.

Inside the dimly lit room and jammed together were chairs, sofas, and tables. From an urn, coffee spewed its aroma covering the sweat of innumerable travelers. This morning the ready room held three people. In one corner, covered with newspapers, slept an Army general no more than 35-years-old.

On the opposite side of the room, two women tried to sleep in the stuffed parlor chairs. Walking softly so as not to disturb them, Eric went to the coffee urn and drew black coffee. There was no milk or sugar, so he accepted the omission and began to sip the hot beverage.

A Negro steward burst open carrying a tray heaped with wax-paper-wrapped sandwiches. The noise woke all three other occupants. The General leaped to his feet ending in a fighting crouch. Realizing where he was, he relaxed.

Dressed in leather airmen jackets, the women opened their eyes for a few moments and returned to whatever sleep cycle they had reached.

Walking over to the urn, the General asked the waiter if there was any milk or sugar. Promising to return with both the left.

"Darby," the General said to Eric.

"Dykman, Sir."

"No formalities here. You going on the bird with those two?"

"Yes, I was told their would-be female pilots.

They're supposed to know what they're doing, but they've been sleeping since I got here."

"So were you."

"Only sensible thing to do until we leave." They said something about 7am."

"That's what my orders read."

"Let's hope it's close to that time."

A booming mid-western female voice shouted at them from one of the chairs. "We're leaving just as soon as they fuel up that buggy."

The voice belonged to the blonde female who appeared at the urn without them noticing. She poured herself a cup and another for her still sleeping co-pilot. Sporting Captain's bars Agatha Sherwood stood just under five feet five and needed shoe lifts to pass the entrance exam for the WAVS or the Women's Aviation Volunteer Service.

Formed to fly Army Air Force planes on non-combat routes, they ferried new bombers to England and Africa, freeing men for combat assignments. Called Aggie, Captain Sherwood was one of the longest-serving WAVS. Already the survivor of two crashes during ferrying flights, she knew a third would permanently ground her from such missions. While there were other jobs inside the WAVS, Aggie savored her trans-ocean trips because of her English boyfriend.

Aggie worked with other pilots to figure out why some planes landed with empty tanks and others reported significant fuel reserves. Little understood during the war, high altitude air streams usually moving easterly enabled flights west to east to more easily complete the crossing.

Unless pilots were prudent, they could find themselves in the ocean instead of dry land when these streams slowed or vanished. Conversely, planes flying east to west encountered headwinds which could have the same negative effect.

Struggling out of her sleep, Della Anna Guardia took her superior's offered coffee, her wrinkled nose displaying her displeasure there was no milk or sugar. Dressed almost identically, the women could have been twins except for Della Anna's dark skin and jet-black hair. This was her third crossing with Aggie, and the women had fallen into an easy division of duties. Della Anna went into the bathroom and locked the door after again with her face indicating no one should follow.

Seeing the men's room sign above her head, Eric realized women didn't have separate facilities. When Della Anna came out, Eric went in to relieve himself, with Darby following.

"Not much of a can on a B-17," he said, unzipping his fly.

"Haven't ridden in one before."

"Keep your oxygen mask handy, sometimes they fly higher and get into the thin air," he added.

"I sleep most of the way with an oxygen bottle nearby."

"Good advice."

"Try to help. Let's get this show on the road."

The room was empty when they came out of the washroom. Both men picked up their gear, grabbed sandwiches from the tray, and went to the tarmac. Still new from the factory, the B-17 was the latest version gaining fame as the G model. No machine guns were bristling from its various defense ports to save weight.

Ground crews were siphoning more fuel into its wing tanks. Separating, the pilots split pre-flight duties. One went into the cockpit;

the other was doing the walk-around inspection. Unsure of how to board the plane, Eric was glad Darby took the lead. The general showed familiarity with the airplane and hoisted himself up into the plane's belly, using the crew's entry port. Eric did the same, finding himself inside the bomb bay. Darby motioned for him to go forward while the General found the only flat place in the rear.

"I plan to sleep my way across," he shouted at Eric.

"Good idea but I don't think I can."

"Then find the radio man's cubby and settle in there. Best spot besides mine."

"You've done this before?"

"In the Pacific, there are long stretches of ocean and you learn how best to make the time go by."

"I don't know if I can sleep."

"You'd better sleep now as they'll keep us pretty busy in England."

"I have a lot on my mind."

"We all do, Captain."

Darby's pointed finger forward, by following it, finding the radio man's cubby proved easy, just behind the pilot's compartment door. Setting his gear down across the aisle in the navigator's nook, Eric sat in the cushioned swivel seat, appreciating the thought that went into its design.

Surveying his perch, Eric realized there was no radio equipment. Puzzled, he made a mental note to ask the pilots about its absence. His unasked questions were answered when Della Anna went past dragging radio equipment, and she paused to smile at him.

"Thought we go across the ocean without a radio?"

"Wondering."

"This unit is 25 pounds when they install their radio it adds 75 pounds."

"Fifty pounds makes that much of a difference?"

"Multiply it over three thousand miles, and the answer is yes."

"If I had known, I would have left some stuff home."

"If things get hairy, we sometimes throw stuff overboard," she laughed.

While not precisely the same, Della Anna's laugh reminded him of Christiana's sly chuckle. Eric winced, hoping the pilot did not notice. If she did, she said nothing but proceeded to the flight deck. Left alone, Eric slumped back onto the seat. Still there 20 minutes later, first one, then two, and three engines roared to life. There was another minute before the fourth engine coughed. Minutes flew by as the pilots adjusted the fuel flow and pitch of the four-bladed propellers. When they were satisfied, the plane taxied to the very end of the runway.

Eric looked out the tiny window in the compartment and saw grass beyond the tip of the wings. The engines reached full throttle with brakes on before they were released, and the plane lurched down the runway. Not noted for its quickness in getting airborne, this B-17 was loaded with fuel as the pilots hoped to avoid stopping in Greenland on their way to Europe.

With the runway petering out, the plane finally rose off the concrete and flew out over Sheepshead Bay toward the northeast. Eric realized the heavily loaded plane was reluctant to gain altitude. He saw the two pilots gently nursing it upward through the open cockpit door, gaining height by the foot.

Staring out of his porthole-size window, Eric tracked their progress as the ocean below receded. They were 200 miles off the coast before the plane passed through the 10,000-foot level. He wondered how high they would go before leveling off. Sleepy, he was sorry now he had foregone the coffee in the lounge.

An hour into the flight, Della Anna came back to him, thermos in hand. Figured you didn't bring any coffee; we have lots up top. Eric took the cup gratefully, drinking it as she made her way to the back.

"Our other guest is asleep," she said, returning quickly.

"He said he would."

"His loss, want some more?"

"No, but where's the can?"

"You see that can there?" she laughed, pointing to one locked in place under his seat.

"I was wondering what that was there for."

"That's yours," she said with a laugh.

"What do you do?"

"We bring wider cans." She laughed as she moved past him to the forward deck.

Savoring the coffee, Eric sat back in his chair, listening to the steady engine drone. His daughter, her grandfather, and then Christiana came to mind in order. Seventeen days had elapsed since her brutal death. His grief was smothered by concerns for their daughter, the search for her killer, and the terrible choice he avoided in New York. Hating himself for not being able to execute her killer, he wondered if that decision would haunt him all his life.

Shivering from the cold, he gathered his sea coat closer to his body. Faintly, from memory, he smelled the perfume Christiana wore the last time she twirled around the room naked. Inflamed, he had dragged her onto the bed and smothered her with kisses. In his lifetime, controlling oneself was always paramount. Yet, in their sexual romps, he lost all control, seeking to catch his wife's essence in these moments. Sadly, he said to himself, he never did.

"Perhaps if we had more years together, I would've learned more," he thought.

On this last note, Eric fell asleep thinking of her and, in his mind, selfishly thinking of all he had lost. Over the drum of the engines, a drowsy Eric thought he heard Christiana's voice. In the dreamlike state midway between arousal and sleep, she was standing outside the radio cuddy smiling that secret grin reserved only for him.

"But you do know me, Nestor," she whispered to him.

"Not as much as I wanted to," he said to the passageway.

"I gave you everything of me," she smiled, tilting her head as she always did when saying something important.

"We did not have enough time," he cried.

"God gives us enough time for the important things," with the severe look she could muster on occasion.

"What is more important than us being together," he almost cried.

"Our daughter, your work, the money you must manage."

"You gave me Alexandra but you didn't stay."

"I couldn't, he hurt me too much. It hurts now."

"I know. I saw you. But I could not kill him."

"Killing him would not bring me back," she seemed to shiver.

"No, nothing will."

"We did have six years," she said brightly and with a slight smile.

"But I was often away."

"True, but when you were home, I knew you were all for me."

"From the first moment I saw you I loved you."

"And I love you even now. That is why I am here."

"You're making me miss you even more."

"You have most of your life to lead, will you remember me?"

"How can I forget you? You are the only woman I will truly love. I will always love you."

"Find other loves Nestor just please don't forget me."

As Christiana faded from his view, Eric felt someone shaking him. Vigorously pushing his arm away, Della Anna replaced Christiana in his vision, trying to put an oxygen mask on Eric's face.

"We've gone high enough that you should put on your oxygen mask. The general has his on and sleeping away, and you need to get yours on pronto. You were mumbling. Are you in the habit of telling people you love them? Della Anna said lightly.

"I was dreaming I was talking with my wife."

"Happens up here if you don't have enough oxygen. You left her behind in the states so you'll just need to settle for dreams till you return."

"Yes, I guess I will need to settle for dreams."

No more dreams came to Eric before, hours later, the coast of Britain came into view. Landing in Northern Ireland for refueling, the crew finally deposited Eric at Stansted Airbase on June 1, 1943. Their orders were waiting for him to report to General Eisenhower's headquarters as soon as possible.

The next day, still adjusting to European hours, Eric met with Ike's number one aide, General Bedell Smith.

"Ike remembers you from some meeting with Admiral King."

"I forgot he was there."

"People don't usually forget Ike."

"I was so scared of Admiral King."

"Heard he was a tarter to junior officers."

"And generals."

"Ike thinks you can solve a problem for us."

"The problem."

"Loading ships in England and off-loading in a combat zone."

"There are a lot of Marines who've done it in the Pacific."

"Ike thinks you can do better."

"Is that why I'm here?"

"It is very important, start today and come back in a month with some answers."

"I'll start today, but I will return only when I have answers."

"Ike said that would be you'd say. Got a British woman something to help you who has been in the transport area. She's outside. Find quarters and get to it we don't have much time."

# September, 1943
## Miriam Brinkerman

Behind the blacked-out curtains of wartime England, desperate men and lonely women found each other. The men seeking to avoid thoughts of impending battles and frigid seas. Many women, newly liberated from their homes by wartime jobs hoping for romance and adventure.

Music, often from female bands, punctuated the stale air of nightclubs, dining halls, and cabarets, drowning out the wailing sirens, strident warning horns, and exploding bombs.

Their hooded lights forced cars and taxis to slowly pick their way through the streets. In one cab, Eric and Miriam Brinkerman huddled against the damp. Both held briefcases stuffed with analysis and recommendations resulting from three months of feverish activity throughout England.

Since his arrival in England, Eric was constantly moving from one ministry to another, piers alongside warehouses, billets, and depots across the nation. After Miriam met him outside his temporary quarters on the morning of his first day in England, were together as much as 20 hours each day. Whether on in their office together dockside on the Thames or on the road, the two were inseparable.

To others in the office building, or those they met in their travels, all thought they were sleeping together. Miriam herself wondered why Eric did not at least try to sleep with her. The man, himself, was still torn-up in his grief to notice stares of wonderment about their relationship. What she did know, Eric was a bear for work. For her, the work enabled her to stop worrying about Ian.

As the day for the briefing meeting drew near, Eric was glad for Miriam's help. Without her knowledge of the ministries, manufacturers, and ship movements, Eric admitted his assignment from Ike would have been almost impossible.

To stretch their days, wartime leaders often scheduled late night conferences. Eric found it amusing to shave and dress at 10pm, and Miriam said she was used to these scheduling quirks. Thanks to Miriam, he was prepared with his charts and recommendations.

Arriving at SHAEF headquarters, the small room they were ushered into indicated the briefing would be an intimate affair. How intimate was evident when only four men entered from the other door. Besides Ike, who joined after Prime Minister Winston Churchill, Eric recognized Bedell Smith. The fourth general, in British uniform, did not introduce himself, and the other personages didn't bother to enlighten him.

Churchill took charge of the meeting in his usual gruff manner and ordered Eric to communicate his findings. For the next 30 minutes, with Miriam's help, Eric presented his plans for loading and unloading war materials and supplies when the invasion of Europe occurred. Eric started his presentation by stating the problem: the loading in England needed to ensure no bottlenecks to unloading in France.

While obvious to everyone in the room, Eric's plans for organizing this effort impressed them. As his presentation progressed, Eric's audience realized he had developed a method that provided the best way of supplying the men on the beach and immediately inland.

Not letting his poker face betray his pleasure, Ike congratulated himself that he remembered Eric's briefing ton Admiral King years earlier. There was silence in the room until Churchill asked some questions, and Eric replied, and the Prime Minister indicated his approval, and the meeting began to break up.

Silent throughout the meeting, the third general spoke up.

"Why are you only a captain? There are others in your Navy with less experience who are Admirals?" he asked.

"Not enough sea duty. My career got sidetracked into cargo handling and convoy routing."

"How are you able to deal with some of our people who are rank conscious."

"With difficulty."

"Have you asked for sea duty?"

"Too busy doing this job. Some of my superiors think it's more important than sea duty."

"I agree. I think we can let this man continue with what he's doing. Don't you agree Mr. Prime Minister?"

Already thinking about his next meeting, Churchill gave a gruff nod and told Ike to handle the details.

"Report to Bedell tomorrow after 1pm, and you'll have your orders," Ike said and walked out with Bedell Smith in his wake. Churchill waddled out the same door, followed by the British General.

"I the other general who I think he was?" Eric said to Miriam.

"Montgomery," she replied.

Exhilarated by the meeting, the couple began putting together the final loading protocols they ordered to prepare the next day. After four months of non-stop activity, their work was almost completed. Ike and his staff were reading their recommendations during the Christmas break.

With nothing to do for the moment, Eric suggested drinks at the nearby Strand Hotel. Tired but equally flushed with success, Miriam accepted. The hotel ballroom and bar were crowded when they arrived. After 20 minutes, a small table opened up, and they sat down. The waiter said they only had gin fizzes because of wartime shortages, so they accepted his pronouncement.

"Seems the only words people have nowadays is "It's the war," Eric laughed.

"First, I've heard you genuinely laugh," Miriam said, smiling.

"How would you feel assigned to answer to that lot we just met?"

"Pretty honored."

"I guess I should but you notice there was no naval presence there."

"They are out there fighting the war."

Laughing out loud, Eric sat back and, for the first time, really looked at his assistant, now co-investigator. That she was pretty, there was no denial judging the looks she got from other men in the room. Long hours on the road, in dingy factories, and on wind-swept docks etched tired lines in her face and hands. Under her regulation uniform was breast and curves men dream about. Experienced in the drawing rooms of England's elite, Miriam carried herself with regal grace.

When the orchestra took its break, Eric leaned across the table and asked about her personal life for the first time.

"My fella's an RAF squadron leader based in Scotland," she replied somewhat boastfully.

"Not fighting Gerry anymore."

"No, thank heaven, he trains the boys now. He was an ace, got hurt, and they seconded him to Scotland."

"So you haven't seen him recently."

"The day before I met you, he went back after one week's leave. It was heaven."

"What did you do."

"Little hotel by the upper Thames. We didn't get out of bed 'til 11 and only because they needed to make up the room. Didn't get to punt on the Thames but walked a lot."

"When do you hope to see him again."

"That's really up to you."

"What do you mean."

"My orders are to stay with you until you don't need me."

"Doesn't mean you can't have leave."

"What will you do."

"Sleep and would you believe my mother-in-law came from the Dales and her grandfather still lives on the country estate, so I might visit."

"You have never talked about your family."

"Only have a seven-year-old daughter left in Washington with my Father-in-law."

"You're divorced?"

"No, widowed," he said with such finality Miriam did not ask another question.

Softening his tone, Eric explained his mother-in-law's English antecedents. They agreed Miriam would go to Scotland that weekend and Eric would visit Antigone's manor in the Dales by the end of the night. They clinked glasses before downing their second gin fizzes. Miriam anticipated her reuniting with Ian Harcourt and Eric to learn more about Christiana's heritage.

When Eric arrived at Antigone's ancestral home, it was a billet for Polish airmen stationed at the nearby temporary airdrome. He found her grandfather in an estate cottage with difficulty, slowly drinking himself to death. Depressed by what he was seeing, Eric went back to London to wait for Miriam's return after two days. For convenience and unaware her family owned the buildings, they were in nearby mews flats situated not far from London central. In fact, from his flat, he could see her unit. Noticing lights were on in her flat, he walked over to see who was there. Miriam opened the door; her eyes were red with tears.

"Don't tell me the pilot ran out on you?" he asked half-seriously.

"Rather he flew out on me," she answered in a choked voice.

"What do you mean."

"He's dead. The blither is dead."

"How?"

"Engine trouble and he bailed out but the parachute ripped getting out of the plane."

"I'm so sorry. When?"

"That's the horrible part. It happened a month ago and no one knew to tell me."

"Didn't his mates know about you?"

"We kept it on the down-low. He had no one to tell and my family wouldn't have approved."

"Why not, he was a war hero?"

"He wasn't Jewish."

"You mean you're Jewish?"

"Yes."

"I'm sorry Miriam but no one would ever think you're Jewish."

"Up until now, I rather enjoyed that. But it kept Ian and me from marrying, and now we never will.

"Why did you not marry?"

"My family would've disowned me but I loved him so."

"Funny, my wife defied her family to marry me."

"Really."

"Yes, she always decided what she wanted and then did it. Nothing stood in her way."

"You never talk about her."

"It's too painful even now."

"My father says that when we share our pain, it somehow becomes more bearable."

"Perhaps for some but it is still impossible for me to tell you or anyone of my loss."

"Losing Ian is one pain that will remain with me."

"See, you know a little about how I feel."

"But I don't doubt I will love again."

"I doubt I will. She was my everything."

"Nobody is their everything."

"You never met Christiana; life was not big enough for her."

"How did she die."

"I can't speak of that now, perhaps another time. For now, how can I ease your pain."

"Hold me."

In the twilight of the summer evening, with double savings hours keeping the sun higher, Eric awkwardly held the crying woman. They moved to her small sofa and remained there for hours as Miriam processed her grief. Finally, she crawled into her bed and slept. Eric sitting quietly in the chair by her side. Before dawn, in his drowsy state, Christiana appeared before him. This time she was wearing the same yellow dress from the Massucci wedding.

"This woman really sorrows, Nestor," the wraith said.

"Losing your loved one is always harder when you don't think they will be gone."

"We thought we had forever."

"At least until our daughter was an adult."

"Think of all the fun in bed we would have had."

"I think only of the days I could not be with you."

"You had your duty."

"But I had you waiting for me."

"I am still waiting Nestor until you can join me."

"I have things to do first."

"I know, but I will be waiting."

"Don't go, stay awhile."

"She's waking up. She needs you now. Goodbye for now."

Rubbing her eyes, Miriam thought she heard Eric talking and wondered who was in the room. He seemed half-awake himself when she looked over to the chair he occupied. Realizing an urgent need to use the hall bathroom, she picked herself over the recumbent figure and disappeared. Her movements stirred Eric awake, and he acknowledged how hungry he felt. When she returned, he used the bathroom and suggested they go someplace for breakfast. Demurring, Mariam offered eggs and coffee, which he accepted.

After they ate, Eric went back to his apartment, really one room and sleeping alcove to change. Deciding work was the best medicine, the two grieving people set out to implement the plan they outlined to the Allied leaders.

# December, 1943
## Eric Dykman

Developing the master plan for loading ships taking part in the D-Day invasion required three months of feverish activity that left Eric and Miriam exhausted as Christmas approached. Fueling their commitment to 20-hour workdays was Miriam's sadness over Ian's death and Eric's endless sorrow. Miriam hid her pain while Eric continued to have one-sided conversations with Christiana's specter.

Putting down the phone after a lengthy conversation, Miriam turned to Eric in their office three days before Christmas.

"Henry Batterson is the only person I can't say no to," she frustratedly yelled at Eric.

"Who is Henry Batterson?"

"The man I worked for before you and who got Ian and me together."

"Sounds like a good man."

"The best. He wants me to join him for Christmas."

"Do you good. Has he designs on your body."

"He doesn't do women. Just does not want me to be alone."

"Good idea."

"I can't go there and relive that Christmas without Ian."

"Good way to discharge ghosts."

"You're hardly the one to talk."

"No. you're right, but then I have more baggage than you."

"Well he's extended the invitation to you as well. So, I'll go if you will."

"It would be better than staying in the city by myself."

"Then it's settled."

"Ring him back and tell them I'm joining you."

"Already said you were coming."

"You were that sure."

"No, just scared of how I would feel without Ian and you're the only one who knows how I feel beside Henry and his people."

Borrowing a jeep, Miriam and Eric drove to Henry's estate, now being managed by the caretaker after his mother's death. In the early afternoon of the warm December day, Henry greeted her warmly and welcomed Eric very heartedly.

"Heard a lot about you from Miriam," he said, ushering them into rooms just released from their furniture shrouds and newly dusted.

"Thought this might help the larder," Eric proffered three bottles of bourbon.

"Tough to get this nowadays. I'll trade it at the officers' mess when I get back to the barracks.

"Thought you might," Eric said as he added two cartons of American cigarettes.

Henry ushered them into the house's grand parlor with a knowing wink. "With mums gone, there's only me and a cook from town. The minister has up and died on us, and my estate manager and his wife are entertaining their son home from the army," Henry said by way of making conversation.

"So just the three of us," Miriam said.

"Actually just the two of you tomorrow through the holiday. I've drawn Officer-of-the-day duty from my Colonel. Seems he didn't like me nipping off last weekend."

"Then why'd you have us up here."

"Couldn't let you vegetate in the city, old girl."

"I think it's a great idea," Eric broke in. "We haven't had a break since September."

"So be it. Send the cook home we'll manage ourselves," Miriam said.

"Agreed," Eric said, anticipating sleeping through much of the holiday.

After a late lunch, Henry left his exhausted guests to pile into their beds with the sun still streaking through the clouds. Miriam and Eric slept for almost 12 hours, waking to the nighttime dimness.

She padded into the kitchen to make tea using her military coat as a bathrobe. Raiding the refrigerator's ham hock, she prepared sandwiches as Eric slept.

Laying the fare on the dining room table, she saw the chairs Ian and she occupied that memorable Christmas. Eyes moistening from the memory, she ran from the room, crashing into Eric in the hallway.

"You're running as if you've seen a ghost," he said half in jest.

"I did see Ian and me in that room," she answered, not pulling away from his encircling arms.

"I don't know whether this was such a good idea of Henry's," Eric said doubtfully.

"He thinks it will help me heal."

"What does he know about losing someone you love."

"A great deal. He was devoted to his mother."

"Mothers are one thing, lovers are something else."

"Sometimes they're both for some men."

"Really, he doesn't seem the type."

"Henry hides it well."

"Anyway, what were you doing in there?"

"I almost forgot. Dinner is served."

"Thank god, I am starved."

Pulling away, she took his hand and guided him into the dining room. Careful to take chairs far away from her former seats, they ate in silence. The sparse meal finished, they brought the dishes into the kitchen, left them in the sink, and retreated to the parlor room.

Only one lamp lit the room, and it was in the far corner away from the wireless set that centered activities. Eric turned it on and managed to find some slow music.

"Henry's thoughtfully supplied some port and sherry," he said, examining the decanters on the center table.

"He's always thoughtful. And probably lonely. My guess is he volunteered for duty to avoid being here for the holidays.

"Then why invite us. Leaving us here alone."

"He knows how wretched I feel. Wanted to give me some closure."

"Reminding you of Ian isn't my idea of helping to forget him."

"You don't understand, I don't want to forget him. He was the bravest, most thoughtful man I have ever known. He made me laugh and he made me feel special and he made me want to do more."

"You're doing a lot now."

"Oh, I'm helping us win the war and what you are doing is enormously important but I have a feeling I was born to do something even greater."

"Than winning this war?"

"Yes more than that. But enough about me, we have been together almost six months and I don't even know the names of your wife or child. I have unburdened a little of my sorrow, now it is time for you to as well."

Thrown into a panic by Miriam's quick change of direction, Eric reached for the port decanter to gain time to think of his answer.

In a reluctant tone, he began: "My daughter's name is Alexandra and my wife was named Christiana."

"They are pretty names," Miriam said to encourage his revelations.

"I named our daughter and my wives came from her mother. I told you she was born and raised here in the Dales. I think my father-in-law never really understood his wife or daughter. He's a smart, good man but out of his depth when it comes to English women. The funny part is he's written me to tell me he's marrying my daughter's English nanny. You would think he'd learn. I think she's pregnant by the way their hurrying the wedding along. My daughter's delighted, she gets to play flower girl. Naturally his sons are livid."

"I just learned more about you than all the time we've been together," Miriam smiled.

"What can I say? I'm a private person. My wife picked me out at an Embassy party in Caracas and the next thing I knew I was married and a father."

"That quick."

"We didn't really have a proper honeymoon. She was in the bathroom most of the time."

"So, you were sorry you married her?"

"Not for one blessed minute," Eric said fiercely.

"How did she die and when."

"Just before I came over. I really haven't had time to mourn her."

"But you talk to her every day. I sometimes see you half asleep mumbling."

"You caught me. She appears to me every so often. Mostly to tell me not to forget her. As if I ever could."

"That's what I think Ian would want to tell me."

"You and I are the type of people who couldn't forget. Even if we found someone else to love."

"Even if we found someone else to love," she said thoughtfully.

On that note, they retired to their rooms at separate ends of the long second-story hallway. Eric woke first in the morning and went to the kitchen to brew tea.

He scouted for coffee but, finding none settled on sharing a pot of tea with Miriam. Eric brought the tea and cups to her door using a platter he found. Hearing knocking, she mumbled permission to enter.

Although they had shared an office, traveled hundreds of miles together, and dined across from each other numerous times, Eric had never seen her without any makeup or jewelry.

As she looked up at him with hooded eyes, he acknowledged how beautiful she was. Her pajamas hung loosely, exposing just the slightest rise of her breast, and it was more provocative than if she were naked.

"Tea," he mumbled, trying to avert his gaze.

"This is wonderful. Tea in bed."

"Sorry, couldn't find any scones, biscuits, or bread for toast."

"We'll need to go into the village soon as they close early on Christmas Eve."

"Is today Christmas Eve, I lost track."

"Fraid' it is and you're spending it with a Jew."

"Well if I remember rightly, Jesus was a Jew."

"And my people have been paying for killing him for two thousand years."

"Let's not talk of war or killing for two days."

"I for one would love that. Now get out so I can change and we can get to the village."

Fortified by the tea, they walked to the nearby village. The local bakery sold them bread, some scones, and other sweets. The butcher could only offer them local lamb chops and meager quantities of hams and bangers as he was almost devoid of meats.

"We should have stopped in our commissary before coming here," Miriam said as they wended their way back to the house.

"We'll make do. It's the company that counts and I've got the best."

Miriam blushed at the compliment, the first personal one Eric had ever made. Always in their relationship, he had praised her abilities. For his part, Eric did not realize what he was saying until he said it. They rode the rest of the way in silence.

They took pains at the house alone to avoid being too close or touching. Thinking they would be spending Christmas apart, Eric's gift buying consisted of the two bottles of bourbon he had given to their host.

Also, thinking they would be apart, Miriam's gift to Eric was the British edition of Jane's 1939 edition, then in short supply because of the war. Filching it from her admiral's desk when leaving his command, she had planned to give it to her host.

That December, Christmas Eve was warm for England, and the double savings time meant light still filtered through the curtains, so no electric illumination was needed. Eric found champagne in the cupboard along with fluted glasses. The cork pop was unnaturally loud in the silent house. Miriam took the proffered filled glass and tilted it towards Eric.

"To a better tomorrow," she said.

"To happier days for both of us."

"Do I really look that sad?"

"Yes, almost as bad as I felt when Christiana died."

"How did she die?"

"Too gruesome to even tell you now."

"How long ago?"

"Last May in New York City."

"Were you responsible for her death?"

"In a way. I brought her to the city. Brought her to an event. Left her alone to go to Boston. Came home and found her dead."

"I am sorry."

"Not as sorry as I have been. I should have protected her."

"We cannot protect everyone we love."

"I should have protected her from evil."

"It surrounds us."

"But I could have killed evil but couldn't."

That's because you're a decent man."

"Decent men kill. Look at this war. Our host is certainly on his way to killing."

"Yes, but if his father was not the man he was and if he were not who he is, he would not be there."

"I should have acted."

"But you didn't and you saved your humanity."

"Traded it for a lifetime of regret."

"I think you would have paid a higher price if you had killed evil. Whoever it was."

"Now I will never know."

"God has a way of giving us other chances to find out who we are."

"It is the first time I have heard you mention God."

"I am a Jew. God is always part of us. A big part. I had forgotten him until losing Ian. Perhaps it is time I find him again."

"When you do, say a prayer for me because I am in need of solace."

"We both are," she said, flinging the glass down and rushing into his arms.

Eric suffered a fierce surge of emotion, breaking the dam of anger, sorrow, and regret he had held pent up since Christiana's death. Kissing each other ferociously, they clung to each other while making their way to her room.

Invoking a passion, he thought only Christiana aroused in him; he ripped her clothes from her body. Driving deep within her, months of sorrow, anger, and frustration climaxed inside her body. Not content the first time, he turned her over and thrust inside her again.

Some moment of fear she was betraying Ian made her protest. These pleas turned to moans of joy as she, too, experienced the flood of release followed by pleasure.

When he finished the second time and lay back on the bed, she climbed on top of him, using her hand to arouse him again. Going astride Eric, Miriam rode him until he came again.

Sliding off him with his cum inside her, she lay beside him as the day turned to night. Neither said a word before falling asleep, not wakening until the sun broke through the curtains.

Looking awkwardly at each other, Eric broke the silence by saying simply: "Thank you."

"It was my pleasure," she said ironically. "I needed that as much as you."

"True, but now we have a whole set of complications."

"Says who. Do you think we're the only ones waking up this morning in strange beds after a night of shagging?"

"No, but somehow I think it is different for us."

"I think not Eric, I think I can now call you Eric."

"Seems strange."

"What did your wife call you?"

"At first it was Eric but when she heard my academy nickname she always called me by it."

"And that name?"

"Ha, ha I don't know if I should tell you, you might think me conceited."

"She obviously didn't."

"They gave me the name Nestor after the Trojan war counselor."

"It fits you but when we're alone it will be Eric. Now come here and do it to be again what you did last night."

"I will, at least I think I can, but first I need what you Brits call the loo."

"Now that you say it, so do I."

Their next round of lovemaking was slower, more deliberate, but Eric could not bring himself to the same sense of abandonment as the night before. It was satisfactory but less intense.

Using up the last of their provisions, they scrounged in the pantry to find ingredients for some form of Christmas dinner, they were forced to settle for spam, jam, and crackers washed down with another bottle of champagne.

"Your host certainly did leave an elaborate larder," Eric laughingly said as they ate the last of the crackers in her bed.

Miriam was naked under her bathrobe, and Eric was clad only in his pajama bottoms. Boxing Day night was fast approaching, and the two lovers had spent the day exploring each other's bodies.

Exhausted, they were debating returning to London when the phone rang. Expecting it to be Henry Batterson, Miriam picked up only to hear the voice of some nameless aide to Bendel Smith.

Listening intently, she said yes twice and hung up.

"SHAEF wants us back for an 8am meeting tomorrow."

"They say why."

"New orders the voice said."

"Well that solves the supply problem. Do we go tonight or early tomorrow."

"Tomorrow, I have plans for your body tonight?"

Their return together went unremarked at their post-Boxing Day meeting. Accepting Eric's recommendations, Ike's staff detailed him to draft more comprehensive orders and deliver them to each invasion command personally.

No one demurred when he requested Miriam's continued assignment with him. Despite their best efforts, it was an entire month before they found themselves where they could romp in bed together.

In March, Eric joined Ike's staff at SHAEF headquarters, taking Miriam. But her status became difficult when rules on handling invasion information were tightened and prevented her from working with him.

Despite his efforts to upgrade her security status in May, she was assigned back to the transportation ministry. In a way, it made their affair easier as they could now fraternize in restaurants and nightclubs.

Sometimes the pressures on Eric needed to be released in the form of dancing or simple dinners out. Miriam enjoyed them because they showed a side of Eric she did not see while working with him.

One night they ran into Eric's WAVE pilot Agatha Sherwood who spotted them inside the Strand restaurant. Towing her English lover, she marched to their table.

"Captain, I see it hasn't taken you long to sample Britain's hospitality," she said in her booming voice.

"Enjoying dinner with a former colleague," Eric managed to blurt out.

"She's more than a former colleague by the way she's playing footsies under the table," Aggie said in bemusement.

"I like to keep his feet warm," Miriam said lightly.

"I'm sure you're keeping more than that warm, honey," Aggie rejoined knowingly.

"Just being hospitable to the Yanks. Join us?"

"Don't mind if we do. This is."

She got no further as Miriam leaped in the arms of Lloyd Seventeen.

"Where's your uniform, Link," Miriam said, nestled in his arms.

"Leave it home when I'm out with Aggie. She likes to get the salutes."

"Hard to compete with a full colonel these days," Miriam.

"Well, actually its Brigadier now."

"Imagine that. I always remember you playing with toy soldiers."

"Still do out at headquarters. Won't let me out in the field anymore. Know too much."

"Where's my manners, this is Captain Eric Dykman. This is Sir Lloyd Heventeen with I don't know how many medals."

"So you know each other?" Aggie broke in.

"For ages, he and our friend Henry Batterson go back years and we were at the same house parties before the war."

"I heard about those parties. I'm sorry I missed them," Agatha broke into the conversation, feeling somewhat put out.

"Actually, some were pretty boring," Lloyd said.

"But some were great fun," Miriam rejoined him.

Turning to Eric, Lloyd said in a low tone he had "heard about the work you're doing and want to say about time. Nothing like landing someplace and finding your ammunition is still off-shore. Sure, helps the Gerry if you run out of ammo."

"Nice to feel appreciated. Sit down and join us."

The rest of the evening proceeded smoothly, with Miriam resuming her easy relationship with Lloyd and establishing for Aggie she was not competing for the nobleman. They exchanged confidences in the lady's restroom, with Aggie admitting her knowledge of Lloyd's wife.

"She enjoys horses in the North Country, and he enjoys riding me in the south," was how she put it to Miriam.

"Lloyd was never the one to let one woman satisfy him."

"You ever try."

"No, it takes someone like you to keep his interest beyond one night."

"What about our yank out there."

"He's still pining for his dead wife. I don't know if I could ever replace her."

"Yeah babe, it's hard competing with a ghost."

"Apparently a ghost who was bigger than life."

"Do you think it's worth the effort."

"For now it's good for both of us. I have ghosts too."

"We all do honey."

They returned to the table, and no more of any substance was said until they parted. Aggie was flying back as co-pilot for a civilian clipper, and Lloyd was headed for Scotland. Miriam and Eric went to her apartment and made love until the morning.

It was May 1, and invasion was in the air. Eric set out for one more tour of the docks while Miriam continued at the transport ministry. But by this time, she was involved with Zionists seeking to send settlers to Palestine.

Her ministry work gave Miriam access to documents and stamps needed to clear ships and cargoes. As Eric's assistant, she now knew how to evade British shipping rules to get guns and other supplies to Zionist groups in Palestine.

After learning of Ian's death, she sought comfort in her Jewish heritage. Miriam's newfound faith was not lost on her father in her rare visits home. Together, they began to forge plans for creating a Jewish state in Palestine.

From this tiny beginning, she became an increasing cog in the efforts to sneak Jewish settlers into Palestine. All this she hid from Eric whenever they met and slept together.

After the Normandy invasion, Eric was busy ensuring supplies reached troops on the Continent during the following six months.

SHAEF headquarters and Bedell Smith appreciated his efforts, and their attempts to raise Eric's rank were bedeviled by his lack of sea duty.

Finally, Ike's direct appeal to Admiral King got him the promotion, but the years in grade left him behind his fellow Annapolis classmates in the rankings that determined promotions.

On December 1, Eric got orders to report to the Philadelphia Navy Yard to join a newly launched cruiser as supply officer. Not knowing whether he was pleased or sad, he met Miriam at the Strand Hotel. Beside her was the same small bag she carried when they went to Henry Batterson's almost 12 months prior.

"I'm optimistic we can go someplace for a few days," she said in explaining the bag.

"My bag is with the porter. Let's find a train and go," he said eagerly.

They ended at the coast, which was still under wartime restrictions but managed to find an officers' billet deserted but for three staff soldiers. Ignoring their stares, they signed in and spent the weekend along the dunes displaying their identity cards four times to guardsmen.

Making love in the dunes made up for the separate billets at night, and they were happy. Eric told her of his impending new assignment as they prepared to leave.

Miriam laughed, explaining she was quitting the service to join her father in his export business. Not mentioned was her new commitment to his Palestine efforts. They hug all the way back to London. Parting at the station, she did not promise to write.

Within weeks, Eric was on his ship headed for the Panama Canal and into the Pacific war. But before it left, Eric was ordered to Washington and assigned to oblivion by Admirals still smarting from his actions earlier in the war. Mariam made the first of many trips to Palestine. When Mariam knew she was pregnant, she told her father the baby was by a slain Jewish partisan, and he doubted her but said nothing. Her parents helped raise the baby until she married Aaron Ben Levi, who adopted her son as his own.

On the birth of Israel, her mother died, and her father never got the chance to visit the country he had helped found. Miriam was his contribution to the country he was most proud of.

Eric's cruiser was detailed to the Seventh Fleet, suffered five kamikaze hits before entering Tokyo Bay after the Japanese surrendered. His cruiser was designated to bring soldiers home during the so-called

Magic Carpet that brought almost one million servicemen home before the end of 1945.

When his ship reached San Francisco, Eric was ordered to Washington and assigned to oblivion by Admirals still smarting from his actions during the war.

# Addenda

Starting with his meeting with the wartime chiefs, Eric became Ike's eyes and ears regarding supply bottlenecks and easements. Starting with loading ships for the D-Day invasion, Eric proved invaluable. When more supplies and equipment were needed to enable the allies to punch out of Normandy, he found substitute landing zones for the still German-occupied ports. As Ike wrote for inclusion in Eric's Navy jacket, he found solutions. Credited with many innovative procedures enabling easier off-loading of supplies, Eric pleased General Eisenhower and his staff.

As the war wound down, Ike interceded with Admiral King to confirm Eric's permanent promotion to Captain despite his lack of sea duty. Ike also convinced King to slot Eric into the process by which the Navy selected Admirals. Despite this endorsement, in the post-war Navy, Eric languished in staff assignments without additional promotions.

During those years, working with other service branches, he became the person used to solve complex issues involving loading and unloading military stores. When General Douglas McArthur planned for the Inchon invasion during the Korean War, he was told to get Eric involved. After helping in the planning of that amphibious assault which faced monstrous tides, McArthur became an admirer. Unusual for him, he wrote the Navy Department to praise Eric's work.

Despite all these actions, it took Ike's, now president, personal intervention to finally make Eric an Admiral in 1953.

An Advanced Peek At Volume 2 of

The
Tide Pool
Trilogy

# Tide Pools And Memories Wash Away

—An Unheralded
Military Hero
in Time of War and Peace

## Book 2

# Don Mazzella

# May, 1945
# Eric Dykman

Yesterday's celebrations of VE day left Navy personnel feeling the job was half done as they returned to their Washington offices. With victory in Europe secured, all eyes turned to the Pacific as war planners feared that taking the Japanese main islands would cost untold casualties. Already, Army divisions were being redeployed to that theater of operations.

Captain Eric Dykman was among the first reporting in that morning. Before leaving for work, he hugged his daughter, Amanda, unusually tightly that morning. She cried out in some pain, not realizing how much her father was again feeling the loss of his wife because he could not share this jubilant moment with her. Apologizing, he sent her off to school promising to spend Saturday all day any way she wished. He knew his seven-year-old daughter would choose something involving art.

At his desk in the Navy Shipyard, he looked at the picture of his smiling wife and sighed.

*"You would have had a great time at the parties last night,"* he said to the picture, *"Everyone was dancing and drinking. I would not have said anything last night."*

*"But I was there, you just didn't see me,"* the picture answered.

Startled by the voice in his head, Eric sat back in his chair. A tear almost escaped him. He was saved by the phone ringing in the outer office. He looked up and saw his Yeoman secretary was not at his desk. Forgiving him because of yesterday's announcement of Germany's surrender, he went to the outer office and answered it himself.

The voice at the other end was chillingly familiar.

*"I would think you'd be an admiral by now,"* the voice said. *"Not yet and not in the foreseeable future."*

*"Always knew the Navy didn't know what to do."*

*"We won a war."*

*"With our help."*

*"Yes, with your help."*

*"Time to pay the piper."*

*"We still have another enemy."*

*"Their done for."*

*"Tell them."*

*"Not my job."*

*"What is your job?"*

*"Make my men happy."*

*"They seem to be."*

*"Won't be if the government doesn't keep its promise."*

*"Things like that take time."*

*"The man is impatient."*

*"He'll need to wait."*

*"But too long."*

*"I don't know what I can do."*

*"Just show your bosses what I sent you six months ago."*

*"Don't know if they'll listen to me."*

*"They may be assholes but when Nestor speaks they listen."*

*"Now that's a name I haven't heard in a long-time."*

*"Don't mean to rake up old hurts. But I only met your wife once, but she was unforgettable."*

*"I don't need to be reminded."*

*"I know, but remember also what I did for you."*

*"You did it for yourself, Tony,"* Eric shouted into the phone. *"Because you didn't have the balls."*

Eric slammed the phone down at that point angry at Anthony "Big Tony" Massucci for telling him the truth. Christiana de la Vega Dykman was raped and murdered by his enforcer Sal Vassallo. Given the evidence of his henchman's guilt, Massucci offered Eric the chance to kill the murderer. The Naval officer could not bring himself to accomplish the deed. Leaving the trussed-up Vassallo, Eric went to England to help smooth the transportation efforts for the D-Day invasion.

Despite his successful efforts and the praise of Army leaders, including General Dwight D. Eisenhower, Eric was recalled to Washington and buried deep in the Navy shipyard offices as the war in Europe ended. Senior officers were angry at his tactics in jumping-starting supply and troop movements to the continent at the beginning of the war.

Among his goals at that time were reducing strife and improving stevedoring efforts in East Coast ports. These efforts led to his developing strong ties with Massucci. When the dock boss's daughter needed to get married, Eric was invited to the wedding. Christiana joined him on the eve of her 25th birthday.

Tragically, the almost insane Vassallo saw her at the wedding and managed to rape and kill her in the Waldorf-Astoria Hotel while Eric was in Boston. Fear of mob vengeance prevented witnesses from formally identifying Vassallo to a savvy New York City detective. Despite his usefulness, the detective showed proof of Vassallo's guilt. Massucci knew then that Vassallo must die. Honoring some unknown code, Massucci offered Eric the opportunity of revenge. Eric's basic humanity prevented his acceptance. This refusal was a constant thorn in Eric's mind.

The price of stevedoring peace was the return to America of certain Mafia figures who had been deported, primarily through the efforts of New York Governor Thomas E. Dewy. The deal brokered through Washington reportedly had the approval of the Governor. Eric wasn't privy to all the details but six months before, he received photostats of an order signed by President Franklin D. Roosevelt outlining the deal and pardoning the men named. His copies were in the safe behind him. Massucci's call was not unexpected. Just not so quickly.

Throughout the morning, staff sheepishly trickled into the office. Eric's responsibilities centered on managing sailing schedules for the regular flow of foodstuffs to Europe. More and more these efforts were directed at getting food to the starving populations in countries overrun by American troops including Austria and the Balkans. Compared to what he accomplished during the hectic days before the war and during its early years, they were relatively simple.

Not so simple was his home life. Christiana's death left a great void, but a brief affair in England revealed to him how much she still was in life. Her picture adorned his desk and was in the drawer next to his bed. Realizing the picture somehow bother his daughter, another copy remained in his bedside cabinet to be brought out only when the child was asleep.

Today, Eric started to think about how American troops would be relocated back to the United States. Not his assignment, he mentally reviewed which ships were currently on the Atlantic ocean highways that could be used to ferry troops home. When his yeoman, Alvarez Montoya, finally arrived, Eric ordered him to find the records for nine ships. When they were on his desk, he arranged them by expected arrival date and mentally estimated how many men each could carry on their return voyage. He then, cut orders for the positioning of foodstuffs and clean uniforms being delivered to their docking areas.

When these were ready, he went down the hall to the Admiral in charge of Navy stores. Eric knew the man was one of the senior officers blocking his promotion. Nonetheless, his concern today was helping to start America's European army home.

*"The Admiral in?" he asked the staff officer who headed the office.*

*"No, went on a celebratory tour last night," was the reply.*

*"So, who's in charge?"*

*"Guess that's me."*

*"I have 10 ships here that in the next three weeks can take about 10,000 GIs back home from France or England."*

*"So, what do you need from us?"*

*"Authorization for supplies and to set up a paymaster in each port."*

*"No can do."*

*"Why not?"*

*"Only the Admiral can and he's gone for two weeks. Don't know if I have the authority."*

*"By the time he comes back most of these men will be on the high seas and he'll be a hero."*

*"You think so?"*

*"Know so!"*

*"Okay, I'm out of here in two months, what can he do? Plus I'll blame you, he hates you enough to pin any problems on you."*

*"I figured as much."*

*"It'll take time to do the paperwork."*

*"Got it done for you, my yeoman is a wiz at them."*

By the time the Admiral returned, a well-placed tip to Navy publicity made him a hero. Not giving any credit to Eric, he was photographed welcoming the first shipload of returning veterans less than a month after VE-day.

For his part, Eric said nothing and continued his Navy career in relative obscurity. Until Secretary of State George E. Marshall called.

# May, 1945
## The General

Whiffs of decaying bodies buried in Dresden's ruined buildings permeated streets devoid of people. Only the shell shocked and opportunist looters roamed during night hours. Civil law order reigned by day, chaos at night.

Military establishments were being abandoned as soldiers decided to leave their posts and go home. At the city's martial center, once an avalanched of activity now patrolled by only one or two guards who called their barracks home.

On the top floor hidden from outside eyes by heavy curtains, three figures remained inside the big set of offices, once the heart of Dresden's military.

Putting the glass of cognac to his mouth caused both his arms to shake. On the side table was the half-full bottle of finely aged liquor, two empty glasses and the gun. Said to be 90 years old, the liquor was from the cellar the French chateau that was his headquarters in the war's early years. Now, the General believed it was the last cognac bottle left in the eeee

A commanding figure even when sitting, the General looked from the bottle to the gun his father carried to war before him. Given to him as a young officer, he carried it through two world wars nestled on his belt. Still serviceable it laid there waiting for one final familial duty.

In front of the general two men awaited orders. Standing stiffly at attention in civilian clothes did not hide their military training. Both were tall but the darker of the two was beginning to show ridges of fat and visages of middle age stoutness. Years of good living in staff positions as the German tide rolled over Europe softened the once hard features. Even in the ebb of fortunes, he enjoyed the best foods and wines. The general bet to himself his last meal in the city was at the best remaining restaurant. Hardship was foreign to this man.

Not an ounce of fat betrayed the second officer. Tough service in France, North Africa, Russia and finally Germany left ridges of scars not eased by extra weight. Never asking his men to do more than he himself was doing, their graves attested to his allegiance to the leader, the party, the army.

Stirring in his seat, the General looked from one man to the next. He respected one, despised the other but trusted them both to fulfill their assigned missions.

*"In the Great War, the English and French airmen counted fellow pilot's death by saying they went west. You are going west to live and keep something alive for future generations,"* the General said in a voice barely above a whisper.

*"You each have a mission. I won't be around to see if you are faithful to your orders, but others will know. Do it well and perhaps Germany will be great again. Fail, and there is no hope."*

The two men clicked their heels together but remained silent.

*"Your orders?"*

The stouter man spoke quietly, urgently, and without emotion.

*"I am to remain here in Germany but only after going west to be interred by the Americans. They are the softer of our enemies and I should be free soon after hostilities end."*

*"Somehow, I must survive until shipping once again revives, then get a job. Preferably in Hamburg. After some period of time, I will open an import-export business specializing in South American trade."*

Although this had been discussed before, the General wanted to review it one more time.

*"How will you finance this venture; you are without a pfennig?"*

*"When I am ready, I will go to Switzerland and talk to a man there. He will advance me the money. When I return my story is an aunt died in Switzerland."*

*"What if people doubt your story?"*

*"That man in Switzerland will give me all the documents I need plus some pictures to show anyone who asks."*

Nodding his head, the General sipped the cognac. It warmed his stomach but did not chill the icy fingers of doubt he had about the whole project. He did not believe this man would remain loyal to the other people in the operation. But brains are needed now and possessing a certain amorality. Only someone like this man who managed to live through six years of war and never hear a shot fired was right for the tasks he was assigned. If he remained committed to the effort, he would play his role well. The General also didn't doubt some monies stayed in his pockets. Compared to the benefits, a small price to pay. Still, he preferred a different choice, if one was available

"How will you remember all these details?"

"One slip of paper sewed into my sleeve!"

Turning to the other man, the General was startled by the flood of emotions. As his student, the General had marked him out in 1936 at the War College. With a Jewish mother, now dead, advancement was hard. With his father, she died in 1938 during a mob rampage in Berlin. Only the General's intercession gave him a chance to excel on the battlefield. Rapid promotion and a demonstrated zeal for the party made his rise to Colonel possible. But for the Jewish blood, he would be a general today

Perhaps it is best he never made general. He has a far more important mission today.

*"Your orders?"*

*"Leave, make my way south to Switzerland and contact a man in Lucerne. Stay there until the war is over. Relocate to South America and blend in with the citizens. Use channels he creates to begin transporting material you will store with him to South America using his Swiss company. Never more than one or two items included with regular merchandise. Then when all materials are safely in South America cut all ties and change identities. Use the funds generated to begin investing in companies there, particularly in Brazil, Uruguay, Argentina, and Chile."*

*"Don't forget to marry well,"* the General permitted himself a small laugh. *"A blond?"*

*"Whatever suits you. Just don't buy an untested cow. Sample the milk first."*

One more sip of the Cognac passed the General's lips. He motioned to the two men to join him. They filled their glasses, almost emptying the bottle. The General stood up, they raised their glasses and drained the contents. As he signaled them to leave, they gave him the Army salute, turned on their heels and left.

The General sat down, reached onto the table and picked up the gun. A shot rang out as the men left the deserted outer office. They did not look back.